e.m.

New York Times best .... in Portmahomack, Scotla .... ur-ing Thomas and Charl .... e-vision. THE CATER S .... d by millions of viewers w .... Also available from Headline .... y's critically acclaimed William and Hester Monk series.

Praise for Anne Perry's novels:

'A beauty, brilliantly presented, ingeniously developed and packed with political implications that reverberate on every level of British society . . . Pitt delivers Perry's most harrow-ing insights into the secret lives of the elegant Victorians who have long enchanted and repelled her'

New York Times Book Review

'The novel has a totally contemporary feel and is admirably well-written'   *Guardian*

'Perry's characters are richly drawn and the plot satisfyingly serpentine. However, the best element in [SLAVES AND OBSESSION] is Perry's depiction of the excitement preced-ing and the butchery during the Battle of Bull, reminiscent of Thackeray's unflinching portrait of Waterloo in VANITY FAIR. A remarkable addition to the Perry canon' *Booklist*

'A complex plot supported by superb storytelling'

Scotland on Sunday

'Master storyteller Anne Perry moves closer to Dickens as she lifts the lace curtain from Victorian society to reveal its shocking secrets'   Sharyn McCrumb

A Christmas Visitor

Anne Perry

headline

First published in Great Britain in 2004
by HEADLINE BOOK PUBLISHING

First published in paperback in Great Britain in 2005
by HEADLINE BOOK PUBLISHING

A HEADLINE paperback

1

ISBN 0 7553 2365 3

Typeset in Times New Roman by
Letterpart Limited, Reigate, Surrey

Printed and bound in Great Britain by
Mackays of Chatham plc, Chatham, Kent

Headline's policy is to use papers that are natural, renewable and
recyclable products and made from wood grown in sustainable forests.
The logging and manufacturing processes are expected to conform
to the environmental regulations of the country of origin.

HEADLINE BOOK PUBLISHING
A division of Hodder Headline
338 Euston Road
LONDON NW1 3BH

www.headline.co.uk
www.hodderheadline.com

A CHRISTMAS VISITOR

To those who are willing to give
the best they have

'There, are yer right, Mr Rathbone, sir?' the old man asked solicitously.

Henry Rathbone tucked the blanket around his legs where he sat in the pony trap, his luggage beside him. 'Yes, thank you, Wiggins,' he replied gratefully. The wind had a knife-edge to it, even here at the railway station in Penrith. Out on the six-mile road through the snow-crusted mountains down to Ullswater, it would get far worse. It was roughly the middle of December, and exactly the middle of the century.

Wiggins climbed up into the driver's seat and urged the horse forward. It must know its own way by now. It had come here most days when Judah Dreghorn was alive.

That was Henry's miserable reason for coming back to this wild and marvellous land he loved, and had walked with Judah so often in the past. Even the names woke

1

memories of days tramping up long hills, wiry grass under his feet, sweet wind in his face and views that stretched for ever. He could see in his mind's eye the pale blue waters of Stickle Tarn looking over towards the summit of Pavey Ark; or the snow-streaked hills of Honister Pass. How many times had they climbed Scafell Pike to the roof of the world, and sat with their backs to the warm stone, eating bread and cheese and drinking red wine as if it had been the food and drink of gods?

Then two days ago he had received a letter from Antonia, her words almost illegible, to say that Judah had died in a stupid accident. It had not even happened on the lake, or in one of the winter storms that raged down the valley with wind and snow, but on the stepping stones of the stream.

Henry stared around him now as they left the town and drove along the winding road westwards. The raw, passionate beauty of the land suited his mood. It was steep against an unclouded sky, snow glittering so brilliantly it hurt his eyes, blazing white on the crests, shadowed in the valleys, gullied dark where the rocks and trees broke through.

It was ten years since the four Dreghorn brothers had last been at home together. The family's good fortune in gaining the estate had meant they could all follow their dreams wherever they led. Benjamin had left his ministry in the Church and gone to Palestine to join in the Biblical archaeology there. Ephraim had followed his love of botany to South Africa. His letters were full of sketches of marvellous plants, peculiar to the country, many of them so useful to man.

Nathaniel, the only other one to marry, had gone to America to study the extraordinary geology of that land, exploring features that Europe did not possess. He had even trekked as far west as the rock formations of the desert territories, and the great San Andreas fault in California. It was there that he had died of fever, leaving his widow Naomi to return now in his place.

Antonia had written in her letter that they were all coming home for Christmas, but what a bitter and different arrival that would be. Little wonder Antonia had wanted her godfather to be here. She had terrible news to tell, and no other family to help her. Her parents had died young, she had no siblings, only her nine-year-old son, Joshua, who was as bereaved as she.

Henry had known her all her life, first as a grave and happy child, eager to learn, forever reading. She had never tired of asking him questions. They had been friends in discovery.

Then, as a young woman, a slight distance of self-consciousness in her had put a distance between them. She had shared more reluctantly, but he had still been the first to learn of her love for Judah, and with her parents dead, it was he who had given her away at her wedding.

But what could he possibly do for her now?

He tucked the blanket closer around himself and stared ahead. Soon he would see the bright shield of Ullswater ahead, and on a day as clear as this, the mountains beyond: Helvellyn to the south, and the Blencathra range to the north. The high tarns would be iced over, blue in the shadows. Some of the wild animals would have their white winter coats, the red deer would have come down to the valleys. Shepherds would be searching for their lost sheep. He smiled. Sheep survived very well under the snow; their warm breath created a hole to breathe through, and the odour of their sweat made them easy enough to find for any dog worth his keep.

The Dreghorn estate was on the sloping land above the lake edge, a couple of miles from the village. It was the largest for miles, containing rich pasture, woods, streams, tenant farmhouses, and went right down to the lake shore for more than a mile. The manor house was built of Lakeland stone, three storeys high, with a south-facing façade.

They went through the gates and pulled up in the driveway. Antonia came out of the front door so soon that she must have been waiting for them, watching at the window. She was tall, with smooth, dark hair, and he remembered her having a unique kind of calm beauty, which showed that inner peace that day-to-day irritations could not disturb.

Now, as she walked swiftly towards him, her wide, black skirts almost touching the gravel, her grief was clearly troubled by anger and fear as well. Her skin was pale, tight-stretched across her bones, and her dark eyes were hollowed around with shadows.

He alighted quickly, going towards her.

'Henry! I'm so glad you've come,' she said urgently. 'I don't know what to do, or how I can face this alone.'

He put his arms around her, feeling the stiffness of her shoulders, and kissing her gently on the cheek. 'I hope you didn't doubt I would come, my dear,' he answered. 'And do everything that I can for as long as it may help.'

She pulled away and suddenly her eyes filled with tears. She controlled her voice only with the greatest difficulty. 'It is so much worse than I wrote. I'm sorry. I don't know what to do to fight it. And I dread telling Benjamin and Ephraim when they arrive. I believe Nathaniel's widow will come too. You don't know Naomi, do you?'

'No, I haven't met her.' He searched her face, wondering what worse news she could have than Judah's death.

She turned away. 'Come inside.' She gulped on the words. 'It's cold out here. Wiggins will bring your things in and put them in your room. Would you like tea, crumpets? It's a little early, but you've come a long way.' She was talking too quickly as she led the way up the steps and in through the high, carved front doors. 'The fire's hot in the drawing room, and Joshua is still in class. He's brilliant, you know. He's changed a lot since you were last here.'

Inside, the hall was warmer but it was not until they were in the withdrawing room, with its red-ochre coloured walls, and the log fire roaring in the grate, that the heat relaxed him a little. He was glad to sit in one of the huge chairs and wait for the maid to bring their tea and toasted crumpets deep in hot butter.

They were halfway through them before Henry broke the mood. 'I think you had better tell me what else it is that troubles you,' he said gently.

Antonia took a deep breath and let it out slowly, then lifted her eyes to meet his. 'Ashton Gower is saying that Judah cheated him.' Her voice shook. 'He says that this whole estate should rightfully have been his, and Judah had him falsely imprisoned, then stole it from him.'

Henry felt as if he had been struck physically, so stunned was he by her words. Judah Dreghorn had been a judge in the local court in Penrith, and the most honest man Henry had ever known. The idea of his having cheated anyone was absurd.

'That's ridiculous!' he said quickly. 'No one would believe him. You must have your man of affairs warn him that if he repeats such an idiotic and completely false charge, you will sue him.'

The shadow of a smile touched her mouth. 'I have already done that. Gower took no notice. He insists that Judah took the estate after charging him falsely and imprisoning him, when he knew he was innocent, all in order to buy the estate cheaply. And, of course, that was before the Viking site was found.'

He was totally confused.

'I think you had better tell me the whole story from the beginning. I don't remember Ashton Gower, and I know nothing about a Viking site. What happened, Antonia?'

She drank the last of her tea, as if giving herself time to compose her thoughts. She did not look at him but into

6

the dancing flames of the fire. Outside it was already growing dark and the winter sunset lit the sky and burned orange and gold through the south windows on to the wall.

'Years ago Ashton Gower's family owned this estate,' she began. 'It belonged originally to the Colgrave family, and the Colgrave widow who inherited it married Geoffrey Gower, and was Ashton's mother, and of course Geoffrey left it to her. It all seemed very straightforward to begin with, until Peter Colgrave, a relative from the other side of the family, raised the question as to whether the deeds were genuine.'

'The deeds to the estate?' Henry asked. 'How could they not be? Presumably Gower's father was the legal owner, on his marriage to the Colgrave widow?'

'It was a question of dates,' she replied. She looked tired, drained of all strength. The story was miserably familiar, even if it was also inexplicable. 'To do with Mariah Colgrave's marriage and the death of her brother-in-law, and the birth of Peter Colgrave.'

'And this Colgrave contested Gower's right to it?' he asked.

She smiled bleakly. 'Actually he said the deeds were forged, and that Ashton Gower had done that in order to inherit the estate himself, when it should have reverted to her. He insisted the case went to court, so naturally in time it came before Judah, up in Penrith. The first time he examined the deeds he said they looked perfectly good, but he kept them and looked again more closely. He became suspicious and took them to a very good expert on documents in Kendal. He said they were definitely not genuine. He would testify to that.'

Henry leaned forward. 'And did he?' he asked earnestly.

'Oh, yes. Ashton Gower stood trial for forgery, and was found guilty. Judah sentenced him to eleven years imprisonment. He has just been released.'

'And the estate?' Although Henry could guess the answer. Perhaps he should have known, but when he had been here before, there had always been better, happier things to talk of, laughter, good food and good conversation to share.

She shifted a little in her seat.

'Colgrave inherited it,' she said ruefully. 'But he did not wish to live here. He put the estate on the market at a very reasonable price. I think actually he had debts to pay. He lived extravagantly. Judah and his brothers all put in what they could, he by far the most, and they bought it. He and I lived here. Joshua was born here.' Her voice choked with emotion and she needed a few moments to regain control.

He waited without speaking.

'I've never loved a place as I do this!' she said with sudden fierce passion. 'For the first time I feel absolutely at home.' She gave an impatient little gesture of her hand. 'Not the house. It's beautiful, of course, a marvellous house. But I mean the land, the trees, the way the light falls on the water.' She searched his face. 'Do you remember the long twilight over the lake in the summer, the evening sky? Or the valleys, grassland so green it rolls like deep velvet into the distance, trees full and lush, billowing like fallen clouds? The woods in spring, or the day we followed Striding Edge up towards Helvellyn?'

He did not interrupt her. To remember the beauty that hurt was part of grief.

She was silent for a moment, and then resumed the story. 'Of course, it's worth a great deal financially as well, even before we found the Viking site. There are the farms, and the houses on the shore. It's easily sufficient to provide for Benjamin, Ephraim, and Nathaniel to follow their own passions.' Her face tightened. 'And now that Nathaniel's dead, for Naomi, of course.'

'What is this Viking site you keep referring to?' Henry asked.

'A shepherd from one of the farms found a silver coin and he brought it to Judah. Judah was always interested in coins, and he knew what it was.' Antonia smiled. 'I remember how pleased he was, because it was rather romantic. It was Anglo-Saxon, from the time of Alfred the Great, who defeated the Danes, or at least held them at bay, in the late 800s. The coin we found might have been part of the "Danelaw" tribute, since the rest of it was Viking silver – ornaments, jewellery and harnesses. When we found the whole treasure there were Norse Irish brooches, and arm-rings, Scandinavian neck-rings, Carolingian buckles from France, and coins from all over the place, even Islamic ones from Spain, North Africa, the Middle East and as far as Afghanistan.' Her wonder stayed for a moment or two longer, then faded as the present intruded again.

'Judah invited professional archaeologists in, of course,' she resumed. 'And they dug very carefully. It took them all of one summer, but they uncovered the ruins of a building, and in it the whole hoard of coins and artefacts. Most of the things are in a museum, but lots of people come to see the ones we kept, and naturally they stay in the village. Our lakeside cottages are let nearly all the time.'

'I see.'

She turned to look at him directly. 'We had no idea it was there when we bought the estate! No one did. And the whole village profits from the visitors.'

'Is Gower suggesting that you did know about the hoard?' Henry asked.

'Not in so many words, but he is allowing it to be understood.'

'What exactly is he saying?' He could not help her to fight the accusation if he did not know the truth, however ugly or distressing. The thought of Judah, of all men, being accused of dishonesty was most painful.

'That the deeds to the estate were genuine,' she replied. 'And that Judah knew it all along, and bribed the expert to lie, so Colgrave could inherit, sell the property quickly and cheaply, because he needed the money, and Judah could buy it, and then pretend to discover the hoard.'

Henry saw at a glance both that the charge was preposterous, and that it could also be extremely difficult to disprove because it rested on no reasonable evidence.

Gower was obviously a bitter man who had been punished for a particularly stupid crime, and now lashed out, seeking some kind of vengeance, rather than trying to rebuild his life into the best he could salvage after many years in prison.

'Surely no one believed him?' he said. 'The expert stated that the deeds were forged, and there is nothing to suggest anyone at all knew of the Viking site. After all, it must have been there for centuries. None of Gower's ancestors knew of it, did they?'

'No! No one had the faintest idea,' she agreed.

'Chance,' he replied.

'I know that. But Gower is saying that we only waited long enough to make it seem as if we didn't know. But it alters nothing, if the deeds were genuine. It is only a small lie on top of a greater one.' Her voice dropped a little. The fire was burning lower and the lamplight softened the misery in her face. 'Can you think of anything worse than to send an innocent man to prison, and blacken his reputation in order to steal his inheritance? That is what he is saying Judah did. And now he is not even here to defend himself!' She was close to losing control. The careful mask, which cost her so much, was beginning to slip.

Henry felt the need to say something quickly, but it must be both helpful and true. False comfort now would only make things worse later, and though she might well understand why he had offered it, she would never trust him again.

'He made these charges before Judah's death?' he asked. The truth of facts was a poor refuge, but it was all he had.

Antonia looked up at him. 'Yes. He came out of prison in Carlisle, straight back here.' Suddenly anger took hold of her. 'Why couldn't he have gone somewhere else, and started a new life where he wasn't known? If he'd gone to Liverpool or Newcastle, no one would have known he'd been in prison, and he could have begun again! I've never seen anyone so filled with anger. I've seen him in the street, and he frightens me.' She looked afraid. Her magnificent eyes were wide and hollow, her face almost bloodless.

'Surely you don't think he would hurt you?' he exclaimed. The lights were exactly as before, and the coals were still hot, but it was as if the room were darker. 'Antonia?'

She turned away from him. 'No,' she said quietly. 'You're asking if he hurt Judah really, aren't you?' She drew in a long breath. 'We'd been into the village for a violin recital. It was a wonderful evening. We took Joshua, even though it was late, because we knew he'd love it. He is going to be one of the world's great musicians. He has already composed simple pieces, but beautiful, full of unusual cadences. He took one of them, and the violinist played it. He asked if he could keep the copy.' Her face filled with pride at the memory.

'Perhaps he will be England's Mozart,' he answered.

She said nothing for a few moments, struggling to regain her composure.

12

'Perhaps,' she agreed at last. 'When we came home it was after ten o'clock. I saw Joshua to bed. He was so excited he wanted to stay up all night. Judah said he wanted to walk. He had been sitting all evening. He . . . never came back.' Again she took a few moments before she could continue. 'A while after, I woke Mrs Hardcastle and we sent for Wiggins. He and the butler and the footman went out with lanterns to look for Judah. It was the longest night of my life. It was after three when they came back and said they had found him in the stream. He had apparently tried to cross in the dark over the stepping stones and slipped. They are very smooth there, and could be icy. There is a slight fall a few yards down where they are jagged. They believe he slipped and struck his head, and the water carried him.'

'Where to? It's not very deep.' Was he thinking of the right place, remembering accurately?

'No, but it doesn't have to be to drown. If he had been conscious he would naturally have climbed out. He might have caught pneumonia from the cold, but he would be alive.' She took a deep breath. 'Now I must fight the slander for him.' She lifted her eyes to meet his. 'It is hard enough to lose him, but to hear Ashton Gower say such evil things of him, and fear that anyone at all could believe it, is more than I can bear. Please help me prove that it is absolutely and terribly wrong. For Judah's sake, and for Joshua.'

'Of course,' he said without hesitation. 'How can you doubt that I would?'

She smiled at him. 'I didn't. Thank you.'

★ ★ ★

Supper was early, and there were only the three of them at the table. Henry did not sit at the head, in Judah's place. It seemed an insensitive thing to do, not only for Antonia, but for the grave, pale-faced Joshua, who had not yet reached his tenth birthday, and so suddenly bereft of his father.

Henry did not know him well. Last time he had been here Joshua had been only five, and spent more time in the nursery. Already he had played the piano and been too fascinated by it to pay much attention to a middle-aged gentleman here for a week in the summer, and more interested in hill-walking than music lessons.

Now he sat solemn-eyed, eating his food because he had been told to, and staring at the space on the wall opposite his seat, somewhere between the Dutch painting of cows in a quiet field, and an equally flat seascape of the Romney Marshes, with light glistening on the water as if it were polished pewter.

The servants came and went with each dish, soundless and discreet.

Henry tried speaking to Joshua once or twice, and received a considered answer each time. Henry had a son, but Oliver was a grown man, one of London's most distinguished barristers, well known for his brilliance in the criminal court. Henry could hardly remember now what he had been like at nine years old. He too had been intelligent certainly, precocious in his ability to read, and as far as Henry could remember, in his taste in books. He

14

had been inquisitive, and profoundly argumentative. He could recall that clearly enough! But that was nearly thirty years ago, and the rest was hazy.

He wanted to speak to Joshua, so as not to appear to ignore him.

'Your mother says you composed a piece of music that the violinist at the recital played,' he observed. 'That is very fine.'

Joshua regarded him soberly. He was a handsome child with wide, dark eyes like Antonia's, but his father's brow and balance of head.

'It did not sound exactly how I meant it to,' he replied. 'I shall have to work harder at it. I think it ends a little soon . . . and it's too quick.'

'I see. Well, knowing what is wrong with a thing is at least halfway towards putting it right,' Henry replied.

'Do you like music?' Joshua asked.

'Yes, very much. I can play the piano a little.' Actually he was being quite modest. He had a certain flair for it. 'But I cannot write for it.'

'What can you do?'

'Joshua!' Antonia remonstrated.

'It's quite all right,' Henry said quickly. 'It is a fair question.' He turned to the boy. 'I am good at mathematics, and I like to invent things.'

'You mean arithmetic?'

'Yes. And algebra and geometry.'

Joshua frowned. 'Do you like it, or is it that you have to do it?'

15

'I like it,' Henry replied. 'It makes a very beautiful kind of sense.'

'Like music?'

'Yes, very much.'

'I see.'

And then the conversation rested, apparently to Joshua's satisfaction.

After the meal, and half an hour by the fire, Henry excused himself, saying that he would like to take a walk and stretch his legs. He did not ask Antonia where Judah had died, but when he had his coat and boots on, and a hat and scarf as well, he enquired from Wiggins, and was given directions.

It was nearly half-past eight, and outside the night was dense black, apart from the lantern he was holding, and the few lights he could see from the village a couple of miles away. The sound of his feet on the gravel was loud in the cloaking silence.

He moved very slowly, uncertain of his way, wary of tripping over the edge of the lawn, or even of bumping into the drive gates. It took a few minutes for his eyes to become sufficiently accustomed to see ahead of him by starlight, and make out the black tracery of bare branches against the sky. Even then it was discernible more by the blocking of the pinpricks of light than the line of a tree. A sickle moon made little difference, just a silver curve like a horn.

Why on earth had Judah Dreghorn walked so far late on a night like this? The cold stung the skin. The slight wind was from the southwest, off the snows of Blencathra. Here in the valley the ground was frozen like rock, but there was no gleaming whiteness to reflect back the faint light. He wound his scarf more tightly around his neck and a trifle higher about his ears, and moved forward on what he hoped was the way Wiggins had told him. He had said the distance to the stream was about a mile.

Judah had not simply gone for a walk – it was stupid to persist in believing that. The recital had been splendid, a triumph for Joshua. Why would a man leave his wife and son after such an event, and go feeling each footstep over the frozen ground in the pitch-dark, for over a mile?

Except, of course, it was a week ago now, so the moon would have been almost half full and there would have been more light. Still, it was a strange thing to go out at all, even in a full moon, and why so far?

He had gone to the stream, and tried to cross over it. So he had intended going even further. To where? Henry should have asked Antonia where the Viking site was. But why would he go there at night? To meet someone urgently, or with whom he did not wish to be seen.

Henry was following some sort of path. If he kept the lantern out in front of him, he could walk at about normal speed. It was bitterly cold. He was glad of gloves, but even with them his fingers were stiff.

Who would Judah meet secretly, beyond the stream, at that time of night? The answer that leaped to the mind was Ashton Gower. If it had been any other man, Henry might have thought he was looking for some accommodation, a bargain regarding the trial and the deeds, and Gower's subsequent accusation, but Judah had never equivocated with the truth.

If, on the other hand, he had taken pity on Gower in any way, he would have done it openly, before lawyers and notaries. If he made any threat, that too would have been plain and open.

Perhaps it had not been Gower, but someone else. Who? And why? No believable answer came to his mind.

The land was rising and he leaned forward into the slight wind. Its coldness stung his skin. He could hear the stream rattling over the stones, and somewhere in the distance a dog fox barked, an eerie sound that startled him so he nearly dropped the light.

He moved very slowly now, lifting the lantern so it shed its glow further. Even so, he nearly missed the path to the stones. The water was running quite rapidly, oily black, breaking pale where the surface was cut by jagged lumps poking through, sharp-edged. Then he realised it was the fall he was looking at. The stepping stones were upstream about thirty yards, smooth, almost flat.

But when he reached them and looked more closely, he saw the rime of ice where the bitter air had frozen them moments after the current had washed over. What on earth had Judah been thinking of to try standing on them? What had absorbed his mind so intently that he had taken such a risk?

Puzzled and weighed down by sadness, Henry turned and made his way back towards the house.

★ ★ ★

In the morning he was woken by the housekeeper, Mrs Hardcastle. She was smiling and carrying a tray of tea. He sat up, startled to see daylight outside. That must mean it was nearer nine o'clock than eight.

'And why not?' she asked reasonably when he protested that she should not have let him lie in. 'It was a long way you came yesterday. All the way up from London!' She set the tray down, poured the tea for him, then went and drew the curtains open. 'Not so nice today,' she said briskly. 'You'll be wanting all your woollies on, likely. Wind's off the water, and there's snow on it for sure. Take the skin off your face, it will, if it blows up proper.' She turned back to him. 'Mrs Dreghorn said to tell you as Mr Benjamin's coming today. Telegraph says he'll be in Penrith by noon, so we'll be going to fetch him, as long as the weather holds off. If not, he'll be having to stay at the inn there, which would be a shame, since he's come a fair distance too.'

Mrs Hardcastle could have little idea of the reality if she could liken a train journey from London to rail and ship and whatever else it had taken for Benjamin Dreghorn to come from Palestine to the Lakes in the middle of winter. But Henry forbore from saying so, since very probably she did little more than read and write. Geography may not have been among her needs.

'Indeed,' he said, sipping his tea. 'Let us hope the weather favours us.'

But it did not. By half-past ten, when Henry set out in the trap with Wiggins, clouds were piling up in the north and west over the Blencathra mountains, shadowing the land and promising more snow. Wiggins shook his head and pursed his lips, and added more blankets for his passengers.

They were at least halfway to Penrith before the sky darkened and the wind rose with a knife-edge to it, and the first white flurries came. Henry had not seen Benjamin Dreghorn for several years and normally would have looked forward to meeting him again, but this time it would be very hard. He had offered to go in order to save Antonia having to be the one to break the news to him. Naturally, when he had set out from Palestine several weeks ago, there had been nothing but happiness in view – a Christmas with his family. The bitterness of his arrival would be totally unexpected.

Henry huddled with the blanket around him and the driving snow at his back as they went the last few miles. He hoped the train had not been delayed. If the snow was bad over Shap Fell, it could hold them up. They would simply have to wait for it. He twisted round in his seat, staring behind him, but all he could see was grey-white whirling snow; even the closer hills and slopes were obliterated.

Wiggins hunched his shoulders, his hat over his ears. The pony trudged patiently onwards. Henry tried to arrange his thoughts so he could tell Benjamin of the tragedy as gently as possible.

In the event the train was no more than twenty minutes after the hour. The snow was beginning to drift in places, but the wind had driven it on the lee side at Shap, and the line was not badly affected.

Henry stood on the platform and watched the carriage doors open and searched for Benjamin's tall figure among the dozen or so people who got off. He was the last to come, carrying two largish cases and smiling broadly.

Henry felt his chest tighten and had to force himself to walk towards him.

'Henry Rathbone!' Benjamin said with unaffected delight. He put the cases down carefully on the snowy platform and held out his hand.

Henry took it, wrung it, then reached for one of the cases to help.

'It's good to see you!' Benjamin said enthusiastically. 'Are you staying for Christmas?' He picked up the other case. 'What filthy weather, but, by heaven, it's beautiful, isn't it? I'd forgotten how incredibly clean it is, after the desert. And water everywhere.' He strode forward and Henry had to make an effort to keep up with him. 'I used to hate the rain,' Benjamin went on. 'Now I appreciate that water is life. You get to value it in Palestine. I can't begin to tell you how exciting it is to walk where Christ walked.'

A blast of icy wind struck them as they turned the corner into the street, and it took a few minutes to exchange greetings with Wiggins, load the luggage and make their way out of the town and on to the road west again.

Benjamin resumed his tale. 'You wouldn't believe the places I've been to, Henry. I've stood by the shores of

21

Galilee, probably the very hill on which Christ preached the Sermon on the Mount. Can you imagine that? I've been to Capernaum, Caesarea, Bethlehem, Tarsus, Damascus, but above all, I've walked the streets of Jerusalem and out towards Golgotha. I've stood in the Garden of Gethsemane!' His voice rang with the wonder of it. Even muffled against the wind and snow his sun-burned face glowed.

'You are very fortunate,' Henry replied, meaning it, in spite of how irrelevant it seemed now. 'Not only to see it, but to be so aware of its meaning.'

'I've brought something very special as a Christmas present for Joshua,' Benjamin went on. 'I'm not sure if he'll like it yet, but he will in time. I've got it in the brown case, that's why I've been so careful with it. Antonia will keep it for him, if necessary. But he must be nine by now. I think he'll understand.'

'What is it?'

Benjamin smiled broadly. He was a handsome man, strong-boned, and he had excellent teeth. 'A piece of manuscript from very shortly after Christ's own time. It is the original of half a dozen verses from the New Testament, just a page, but can you imagine how the man who wrote it must have felt?' His voice rang with enthusiasm. 'It's in a carved, wooden box. Beautiful work. And it smells marvellous. They told me it was the odour of frankincense.'

'I am sure he will like it,' Henry responded. 'If not just yet, then in a year or two.'

'Wait until Judah sees it,' Benjamin said eagerly.

Henry could leave it no longer. Not to speak now would amount to a lie. He turned sideways, the wind making his eyes water.

'Benjamin,' he began. 'I came to meet you personally, not only because I am pleased to see you, but because I have some very hard news which I wanted to spare Antonia from having to tell you herself . . .'

The light and the joy drained out of Benjamin's face. Suddenly his blue eyes were bleak and the biting cold of the snow and the wild, colour-bleached landscape seemed hostile, the chill of it reaching into the bones.

Henry did not wait. 'Judah died in an accident eight days ago. He went out at night and slipped on the ice of the stepping stones crossing the stream.'

Benjamin stared at him. 'Died! He couldn't have – it's only a couple of feet deep at the most, if that!' he protested.

'He must have hit his head on the stones.' Henry did not go into any more detail. The explanation made no difference to the truth of it.

'What was he doing out at night?' Benjamin demanded. 'There's nothing there!'

'No one knows,' Henry replied. 'He just said he wanted to stretch his legs before going to bed. He had taken Antonia and Joshua to a recital in the village.'

'It doesn't make sense!'

Henry did not argue. He knew better than to say that such unexpected tragedy seldom did.

Benjamin turned forward and stared into the snow-storm, his face immobile, marked with uncomprehending grief. How could the whole world change in an instant, and with no warning?

They rode for at least another mile without speaking again, and were rounding the last curve in the road when the snow eased and a blue patch appeared in the sky. A bar of light like silver shone on the flat surface of the lake, so brilliant it dazzled the eyes. The village itself was almost invisible with its white-blanketed roofs.

If Henry were to tell Benjamin about the accusation, and save Antonia from having to do it, then he had little time left.

'Benjamin, that is not all I have to tell you before we reach the house,' he said. 'I would prefer that Antonia, who told me, did not have to go through it all again.'

Benjamin turned slowly. 'Judah's dead. What else can there be?' His face was full of pain. He had loved his brother profoundly, and his admiration for him had been intense. The only thing worse than having to tell him of Gower's accusation would be having him find out from someone else.

'Ashton Gower is saying that Judah imprisoned him wrongly, in order to be able to buy the estate,' Henry said simply. 'It is nonsense, of course, but we need to find a way to force him to retract the accusation, and never repeat it again. It is causing much distress.'

'Ashton Gower is in prison, where he belongs,' Benjamin replied a trifle coldly. 'Exactly who is it that is spreading these lies? I'll put a stop to it, by law, if necessary.' He spoke forcefully. He was a powerful man, as were all the Dreghorn brothers, but he had a remarkable intellect as well. He had succeeded brilliantly at university and it was something of a surprise to his family when he had chosen to study theology. But then when his income from the estate had freed him from the need to earn his way, and he had followed his scholastic dreams to the Holy Land, everyone had found it quite natural.

'Gower has served his sentence,' Henry corrected him. 'He is free, and unfortunately has chosen to come back to the Lakes.'

'When?'

'About a month ago.'

'Then I'll go and see him myself. I'm surprised he hasn't been run out of the village. What kind of a man slanders the dead, and adds to the bereavement of a widow and her child? He's less than filth!'

'He is a deeply unpleasant man—' Henry began.

'He is a convicted forger and a would-be thief!' Benjamin retorted. 'If it hadn't been for Colgrave he'd have got away with it.'

'But he made his accusations when Judah was still alive,' Henry finished. 'I don't believe he has repeated them publicly since then, but no doubt he will do. He is determined to clear his own name.'

Benjamin gave a bark of laughter and his face set hard and angry.

There was no more time for conversation. They

approached the gates of the estate and Henry climbed down to open them, then close them after the trap. He walked behind them up the gravel to the door just as Antonia came out.

Benjamin leaped out of the trap, strode the couple of paces over to her, and took her in his arms, holding her gently, as if she were a hurt child.

Then he looked up and saw Joshua standing in the front doorway, dwarfed by the massive lintels and looking embarrassed and unhappy.

Benjamin let go of Antonia and walked up the step. For an instant he seemed uncertain how to treat Joshua. He hesitated, torn between taking him in his arms or grasping him by the hand.

Joshua gulped, standing perfectly still. 'Hello, Uncle Benjamin,' he said very quietly.

Benjamin kneeled down. 'Hello, Joshua.' He held out his arms, and the child allowed himself to be embraced, then after a long moment, very slowly returned it, sliding his arms around Benjamin's neck and laying his head on his shoulder.

Henry found himself overcome with emotion also, and turned away to Antonia. He offered her his arm up the steps, and Wiggins followed with Benjamin's cases.

The following morning Henry got up early because he did not want to lie in bed thinking. When he reached the dining room he found Benjamin already there, with a plate of Cumberland sausage, eggs and bacon and thick, brown toast on the side. Instead of marmalade there was a dark, rich jam in the dish. He remembered from the past that it was wetherslacks, a tart kind of small plum, known as a damson in the rest of England, and Benjamin's favourite.

Benjamin gave him a tight, miserable smile. 'Good morning, Henry. I'm going to see Colgrave this morning. It must have snowed most of the night; it's pretty deep. We can ride. It's only a couple of miles or so. He's an oily swine, and if he had an ounce of decency he'd have stopped Gower already, but we might be able to put a little backbone into him.' He took another mouthful from his plate. 'Or make him more frightened of us than of whatever he thinks Gower will do to him. Ephraim should be here any day, but you can't tell how long it will take to sail from South Africa. What a terrible homecoming!'

'Antonia is expecting Naomi too,' Henry told him.

'I doubt she can help.' Benjamin's broad shoulders slumped. 'I still miss Nathaniel. What's happening to us, Henry? Judah was the oldest, and he was only forty-three, and two of us are dead already! Joshua's the only heir to the Dreghorns.'

'So far,' Henry agreed.

Benjamin did not answer the remark. 'Have some breakfast,' he said instead. 'You can't go out in this weather without a good meal inside you.'

And in spite of the fact that it was only just over a mile and a half to Peter Colgrave's house, it was not an easy journey. The snow had drifted in the night and in places was over two feet deep.

They rode towards the lake and crossed the stream lower down where there was a rough bridge made of two long slabs of stone balanced at either end, and on a central stone. On foot, one balanced with care, but on horseback it was a matter of splashing through, more than hock-deep, and up the other side.

Half a mile beyond they saw the square-towered stone church and the vicarage, then a hundred yards further was Colgrave's house, also of stone. It was handsome, deep-windowed, the roof immaculately slated. One could see where the money from the sale of the estate had been used to repair and extend it, and to build new stables. That was where they left their horses.

'Come in,' Colgrave said, covering his surprise and considerable reluctance with an effort. 'Good to see you, Dreghorn. My deepest condolences on your brother's death. Terrible thing.'

'Thank you,' Benjamin said briefly. 'You remember Henry Rathbone, don't you?'

'Can't say that I do,' Colgrave answered, looking Henry up and down, trying to place his lean figure and mild, aquiline face. 'How do you do, Mr Rathbone?'

Henry replied, finding it difficult to smile. Colgrave was broad, tending to fat a little, although he was no more than forty at the most. He had dark brown hair and a clever, thoughtful face, somewhat guarded in expression.

'Come in, gentlemen,' Colgrave invited, ushering them

through a wood-panelled hall decorated with fine portraits of men and women who were presumably his ancestors. The fire was already burning well in his study and the room was warm. The shelves that lined the walls were stocked with leather-bound, gold-lettered books. 'What may I do for you?' Colgrave asked. 'Anything I can, to be of assistance. You will be returning to the East? Palestine, isn't it? Must be fascinating.' This was directed to Benjamin. He considered Henry to be of no importance, merely a friend brought for company, and perhaps that was close enough to the truth.

'Not until I have cleared my brother's name,' Benjamin said bluntly.

'Oh!' Colgrave let out his breath. 'Yes. Fearful business.' His face tightened in distaste. 'Gower is a total outsider, quite appalling. The man is a fraud, a cheat, and now slanders the name of a good man. Pity we can't set the dogs on him, but we can't.' He gave a slight shrug of his heavy shoulders.

'If it were as simple as that, I should not need your help,' Benjamin retorted. 'You saw the original deeds that he is saying were genuine.'

Colgrave raised his eyebrows. 'Of course. They were so badly forged I don't know how anyone believed them for a moment, except that I suppose many of us are not familiar with such papers, and we are not in the habit of suspecting our neighbours of such a stupid crime.'

'But you would swear that they were forged?' Benjamin pressed.

29

'My dear fellow, I did! In court. Not that it rested on my testimony alone, of course. There was an expert from Kendal, came and also swore they were complete forgeries from beginning to end. We all knew that.' He waved his hand. 'This will blow over, you know. No one with any sense at all believes Gower. The only ones who ever listen to him are newcomers. There are half a dozen families, one or two with money, I admit, who weren't here at the time, so they don't understand.'

'Who are they?' Benjamin asked.

'Leave it alone for a while,' Colgrave said soothingly. 'I'll speak to them on your behalf, and tell them the truth of the thing. Go now, in hot blood, and you'll only make enemies of them. No one likes to be shown up for a fool, you know?'

'A fool?' Benjamin asked.

'Certainly, a fool. Who but a fool would believe a convicted forger like Ashton Gower? They'll learn the truth of him soon enough. Wait until he loses that foul temper of his with them! Or borrows a horse and brings it home lame, as he did with poor Bennion, or tries to borrow money we all know he'll never return. Then they'll wish they'd had more sense than to give him a moment's credence. As angry as you are – quite rightly, of course – you'll make enemies of them now.'

Henry disliked having to agree with Colgrave, but honesty gave him no choice. They excused themselves and left, but as soon as they were outside Benjamin turned around.

'Before we get the horses, I want to go to the church-yard.' He took a deep breath, his face bleak and half turned away. 'I must see Judah's grave.'

'Of course,' Henry agreed. 'So must I. Or would you rather be alone?'

Benjamin hesitated.

'I'll wait,' Henry said quickly. 'I can go later. I'll fetch the horses, then we don't have to go back.'

Benjamin nodded, unwilling to commit himself to speech, but his gratitude was in his eyes.

Henry stood still for a moment or two, watching him walk slowly, crunching through the snow, until he reached the stone wall of the churchyard, and then was lost behind the yew branches.

He went back to the stable yard, and by the time he returned, Benjamin was waiting for him.

'I want to see Leighton, if he's still the doctor here,' he said, taking his horse from Henry and mounting. 'If not him, then whoever is. I don't know how Judah could have been stupid enough to slip on the stepping stones. He's lived here all his life. Where was he going, anyway? What was he doing crossing the stream alone at that time of night? Why did he go out at all?'

'I don't know,' Henry admitted, keeping the horses in step, side by side as they rode towards the village. 'Are you sure it matters now?'

Benjamin looked at him sharply. 'Of course it matters! It doesn't make any sense. There's something wrong, and I intend to get to the truth. Ashton Gower has to be

31

silenced, and permanently. We can't leave Antonia living in fear that he'll start up again.' He was angry with Henry for not understanding; it was clear in his face and the tone of his voice.

Grief and confusion were wounding him and Henry understood that. Still the response stung, and it was an effort to control his own reaction. He had liked Benjamin all the years he had known him, as much as he had liked Judah, and the sense of loss incurred was no stranger to him. It was many years since his wife had died, but the memory was still there.

It was still snowing very lightly but the wind had dropped. Fifteen minutes later they were at the doctor's house and left the horses by the gate. It was another quarter of an hour before he was free to see them.

'Terribly sorry,' he said to Benjamin. 'Dreadful thing to happen. Good of you to come up, Rathbone. What can I do for you?' He was a thin man, full of nervous energy but with a grave voice, nearer Henry's age than Benjamin's.

Benjamin's face was slightly flushed, as much with helpless anger as the sharp edge of the cold outside. 'There's a lot about Judah's death that makes no sense,' he replied. 'I wanted to find the truth of what happened.' He stood in the middle of the room, lean, broad-shouldered, skin burned brown by the sun of the Holy Land, his face hard.

Leighton had been a country doctor for twenty years. He understood grief and the anger that prompted men to fight it. He leaned against the bookcase and regarded

Benjamin seriously. 'The facts are simple. Judah went out for a walk at about half-past ten in the evening. There was a half-moon, but it was still extremely dark. He took a lantern, which was found washed up on the banks of the stream a few yards from where he was. When he did not return home, some little while after midnight, Antonia became sufficiently alarmed to send out the male servants to search for him. They found his body caught in the rocks of the fall a short distance below the stepping stones.'

'I know all that!' Benjamin said impatiently. 'Henry told me. What was he doing there? Why did he go out at all? Why did he try crossing icy stepping stones at night? Where was he going? How does a strong man drown in two feet of water? The stream isn't running fast enough to sweep anyone off their feet, even at this time of the year. I've fallen off those stepping stones a dozen times, and got no worse than wet clothes!'

'You can fall off a horse a hundred times and get no worse than bruises, or a broken collar bone,' Leighton said reasonably. 'But the hundred and first fall can kill you. Benjamin, don't look for reasons where there are none. He slipped in the dark and fell badly. He struck his head on the stones and it knocked him senseless. If it hadn't, no doubt he'd have climbed out and walked home again. Tragically, it did.'

'How do you know he struck his head when he fell?' Benjamin challenged. 'How do you know no one struck him?'

33

Leighton's face darkened. 'Don't start thinking like that, Benjamin,' he warned. 'There's no evidence to suggest anything of the sort. Judah slipped. It was a tragic accident. He drowned. The stream carried him down to the fall, and—'

'You examined him?' Benjamin interrupted.

'Of course I did.'

'What did you find, exactly?'

Leighton sighed. 'That the cause of death was drowning. There were several abrasions on his head and shoulders, one where a smooth stone had struck him, which would be when he fell, several others rougher, where the current carried him down on to the fall.'

'Are you sure it was those stones?' Benjamin persisted.

'Yes. The wounds had little bits of riverweed in them, and his hands were scraped by the gravel at the bottom.' His face was sad and patient. 'Benjamin, there's nothing more to it than I've told you. Don't look for reasons or fairness in it. There aren't any. It is an unjust tragedy, the death of a good man who should have lived a long and happy life. These things happen, probably more often than you know, because it doesn't hit you like this unless it was someone you loved. People die on the mountains, there are boating accidents on the lakes, falls in the hunting field. I'm sorry.'

'But why was he out crossing the stream in the middle of the night?' Benjamin could not let it go.

Leighton frowned. 'Nobody knows that. I don't suppose we ever will. Look to what matters now. Help

Antonia to come to terms with it. Be a support to her, and do what you can for young Joshua. They need your strength now, not asking a lot of questions to which we'll find no answers. And even if we found them all, they would make no difference to what happened. Make the best of what is left.'

Benjamin looked bewildered. 'And Ashton Gower?' he demanded angrily. 'Who is going to silence him? I swear by God, if he goes on blackening Judah's name, I will! And if he had anything to do with Judah's death, anything at all, I'll prove it and I'll see him hang!'

Leighton's face was grim. He straightened up, frowning. 'You can be forgiven a certain amount for the shock of your loss, Benjamin, but if you suggest, outside this room, that Gower had anything to do with your brother's death, you will be even more guilty of slander than he is. There is nothing whatever to indicate that he met Judah or had any intention of harming him, then or at any time. Please don't bring any more grief on your family than it already has. It would be utterly irresponsible.'

Benjamin stood without moving for a long moment, then turned and strode out, leaving the door swinging behind him.

'I'm sorry,' Henry apologised for him. 'Judah's death has hit him very hard, and Ashton Gower's charges are vicious and profoundly wrong. Judah was one of the most honest men I ever knew. To blacken his name now is an evil thing to do. I agree with Benjamin completely and, regardless of what he does, I will do all I can to protect

Judah's widow and son from such calumny.'

'Everyone in the village will,' Leighton said gravely. 'Gower is a deeply unpopular man. He's arrogant and abrupt – we all remember what he did over the forged deeds. But if Benjamin accuses him over Judah's death, he will make it a great deal more difficult than it has to be, because some are then going to see injury on both sides, and it will become a feud, and split the village. That kind of thing can take years to heal, sometimes generations, because people get so entrenched, other grievances are added, and they can't turn back.'

'I'll speak to him,' Henry promised. Then he excused himself and went outside into the snow to catch up with Benjamin.

Benjamin was standing holding both the horses. He looked at Henry defiantly, his blue eyes burning. 'I know,' he said before Henry could speak. 'I just hate being told by that satisfied, self-righteous . . .' He stopped. 'It's thirsty work walking in this. Let's go to the Fleece and take a pint of Cumberland ale. It's a long time since I've tasted a jar of Snecklifter. It's too early for lunch, or I'd have had a good crust of bread and a piece of Whillimoor Wang. There's a plain, lean cheese for you to let you know you're home. I'd like to hear a tale or two of good men and dogs, or even a fanciful yarn of demons and fairies, such as they like around here. They used to write that in as cause of death sometimes, you know? Taken by fairies!'

Henry smiled. 'That must have covered a multitude of things!'

Benjamin laughed harshly. 'Try explaining that to the constable.'

An hour later, warmed and refreshed, entertained by taller and taller stories in broad Cumberland dialect, they emerged into the street again to find the weather brighter, and the sun breaking through wide rifts in the clouds, dazzling on the snow and reflecting on the lake in long blue and silver shards.

They had ridden barely a hundred yards, past small shops, the smithy, the cooper's yard, and were just level with the clog shop where the clog maker was hollowing out the wooden soles with his long, hinged stock knife when they almost ran into a broad-shouldered man with densely black hair.

The man was on foot and Benjamin looked down at him with an expression of cold fury. The man's eyes were narrowed, hard with loathing as he stared back. Henry did not need to be told that this was Ashton Gower.

'So you've returned from following the footsteps of God!' Gower said sarcastically. 'Much good it'll do you. I'll give you a decency of mourning, for the widow's sake, though those that profit from sin are as guilty of it as them that do it. But I suppose a woman's got to stay by her man, she's little choice. It'll make no difference in the end.'

'None at all,' Benjamin agreed harshly. 'Speak another word against my brother, and I'll sue you for slander and see you back in prison, which is where you belong. They should never have let you get out.'

'Slander's a civil suit, Mr Dreghorn,' Gower replied, glaring up at him. 'And you'd have to win before you could do anything to anyone. I've no money to pay you damages. You and your kin have already taken everything that was mine. You can't rob me twice, even if you could prove I was lying, which you can't, because every word I say is the truth.'

Henry tensed, afraid Benjamin might lunge at him, even mounted as he was.

But Benjamin did not attempt to strike Gower. He sat quite still in the icy air. 'The pity is that I cannot slander you, Gower,' he replied. 'Nothing I could say about you is untrue. You are proven a liar, a forger and a would-be thief. You only failed at it because you were so clumsy, so damned bad at forgery that they could see at a glance that the deeds were rotten. You didn't even do it well!'

Gower's face flushed dull red, his eyes like black holes in his head. Now it was he who looked for a moment as if he would find it impossible to control his physical desire to lash out, even grasp at Benjamin and pull him off his horse. He moved, his arm out, then stopped.

'Is that what happened to Judah?' Benjamin asked, his voice grating between his teeth. 'He called you a failed thief, and you lost your temper?'

Slowly Gower relaxed and a slow smile spread across his face. 'I'm not sorry he's dead, Dreghorn, I'm glad. He was a corrupt man, an abuser of power and office, and there's not much worse than a judge who uses his position to steal from the men who come before him believing they'll receive justice. If the judge himself is rotten at the heart, what hope is there for the people? That is a high sin, Dreghorn. It stinks to heaven.'

He stepped back, lifting his head. 'But I did not kill him. He wronged me bitterly. He sent me to prison for a crime I did not commit, and he stole my inheritance from me, as well as eleven years of my life. I spoke against him, and I shall do so as long as I have breath, but I never raised my hand, or told any other man to. As far as I know, it was a just God who finally punished him. And if I wait my time, and plead my cause before the people, perhaps He'll give me back what's mine as well.'

'Over my dead body!' Benjamin said bitterly. 'I'll not accuse you of murder until I can prove it, but then I will. And I'll see you on the end of a rope.'

'Not if there's any justice under heaven, you won't,' Gower retorted. 'I didn't kill him.' And with a harsh, sneering smile still on his face he strode past them through the snow back towards the centre of the village, the wind off the lakeshore tugging at the tails of his coat.

Benjamin watched him until he was out of sight, then he and Henry rode back towards the estate.

'I love this land,' he said after a little while. 'I'd forgotten how good it feels. I couldn't bear it to be poisoned by that man. The idea that Judah would be dishonest in anything is absurd. What can we do about it, Henry? How do we stop him saying these things?'

Henry had been dreading that question. 'I don't know. I've been trying to think of a way, but after meeting

Gower, every sort of reason seems doomed to failure. He has convinced himself that the deeds were genuine.'

'That's ridiculous!' Benjamin said abruptly. 'They were not only forgeries, they weren't even good ones. The expert swore to it, but anyone could have seen it when one looked. Gower's just so corroded with hatred he's lost his wits. Maybe prison has turned his mind.' He looked at Henry. 'You don't think he's a danger to Antonia, do you?'

Henry did not know how to answer honestly. He would like to have said something reassuring, but there had been a wild hatred in Ashton Gower that defied reason. He had no doubt that the man was guilty of forging in a stupid attempt to get the estate. Even if Henry had not known Judah, there was the testimony of the experts about the deeds. Perhaps Benjamin was right, and Gower had lost his mental balance in prison. Heaven knows, he would not be the first man to do that.

'Henry!' Benjamin said sharply.

'I don't know.' Henry was forced to be honest. 'I think we should warn Antonia. The servants must be told. The house must be locked securely at night. You have dogs – they would warn of anyone who should not be around. It may all be unnecessary, but as long as Gower remains in the area, and in the frame of mind he is, I think it would be better to be cautious.'

Benjamin stopped, reining in his horse hard, and turning in the saddle. 'Do you think he murdered Judah?'

It was a jarringly ugly thought, but it had been on the

edge of Henry's own mind too. 'I really don't know,' he admitted. 'I think he is an evil man, and possibly a little mad. But better we should take preventions we don't need than that we should fail, and regret it afterwards when it is too late.'

'How can we warn Antonia without frightening her?'

'I don't believe we can.'

'But that's ... God damn Gower!' Benjamin swore savagely. 'God damn him to hell!'

It stopped snowing in the evening, and a hard wind blew down the lake, whining in the eaves and rattling the windows. But in the morning when Henry pulled the curtains, even before Mrs Hardcastle came with tea, there were bare patches on the north and west faces of the hills, and lower down the snow had drifted deep against walls and fences.

The postmaster arrived after breakfast with a telegraph message from Ephraim, sent the day before from Lancaster, to say that he would be arriving on the midday train. The lawyer also rode up from the village, before going on to Penrith, to speak about the estate to Antonia and Benjamin. Therefore it was again Henry who stood on the platform when the train came in, belching steam into the air, and nearly an hour late because of snow drifting over Shap Fell.

He saw Ephraim immediately. He was as tall as Benjamin, but leaner. And he walked with a loose, easy gait in spite of the cold. He carried only one case; it was quite large, but in his hand it seemed to have no weight at all. Like Benjamin he was burned by the sun and wind, and frowned very slightly as he saw no one he was expecting on the platform waiting for him. He glanced up at the sky, perhaps fearing the snow had been worse here, and he would not be able to go further until it cleared.

'Ephraim!' Henry called out. 'Ephraim!'

Ephraim turned, startled at first, then his face lit when he recognised Henry, and he dropped the case and came forward to clasp Henry's hand.

'Rathbone! How are you? What are you doing here? You've come to stay with us over Christmas? That's wonderful. It's going to be like old times. You look cold, and sort of pinched. Where is everyone? Where's Judah? Have you been waiting long?'

'Not on the platform,' Henry answered with a smile. 'I've been at the inn with a pint of Cockerhoop.' That was the light ale that was so popular locally. He felt a lift of gratitude that Ephraim could welcome him so generously at what had been intended as a family reunion. He was, after all, not a Dreghorn, merely Antonia's godfather, an honorary position, not one of kinship. He dreaded having to tell him the real reason he was here; his stomach knotted up and his throat was tight. Was it better to crush his pleasure immediately with honesty, or allow a little time, let him take joy in homecoming first?

Ephraim was smiling broadly. He was quieter than his brother, a man of deep thoughts he shared seldom, and great physical courage. Whatever fears or doubts he had about anything, he mastered them without outer show. But after being in Africa for four years, the sight of his beloved lakes again woke a joy in him that found expression easily.

'Sounds perfect,' he said with enthusiasm. 'We'll go for some long walks in the snow, climb a bit even, and then sit by a roaring fire and talk about dreams and tell each other tall stories. I've got a few. Henry, there are things in Africa you wouldn't believe!' He picked up his case and matched Henry stride for stride out to the waiting trap, which Wiggins had brought around ready when he heard the train draw in.

'How's Judah?' Ephraim asked as soon as they were in the trap and moving. 'Have you heard from Ben yet? And Naomi? Is she coming too?' There was an eagerness in his voice when he mentioned her name, and he turned away as if to guard the emotion in his eyes from being seen.

Thoughts teemed through Henry's mind, an awareness that there was a new dimension he had not even thought of, and pain he would not be able to read in Ephraim as well as he had in Benjamin, depths he could neither understand nor help. And yet there was no alternative. Now was the moment.

'Benjamin is already here.' He answered the easiest question first. 'He arrived two days ago . . .'

Ephraim turned towards him, blue eyes puzzled. 'Is he all right?'

'No,' Henry said frankly. 'We are none of us all right. Judah died in an accident ten days ago.' He looked at

Ephraim's face as the shock struck him – disbelief, then pain. 'I am sorry I am the one to tell you, but the lawyer called by this morning regarding certain estate matters, and Benjamin stayed with Antonia to see him.'

'Hunting?' Ephraim said hoarsely. Judah seldom hunted, but it was the only way to keep foxes down in the Lakeland, and they devastated sheep if left. Ewes and lambs had their throats torn out; whole flocks of chickens could be slaughtered.

'No,' Henry replied, and told him briefly all they knew so far.

Ephraim huddled into his coat as if suddenly the wind cut through it and it was no protection to his body. 'Where on earth was he going?' he asked huskily. 'At night?'

'We don't know. He said it was just to get a little air before going to bed. They had all been at the village listening to a visiting musician. A violinist. He had actually played a small piece Joshua had written.'

'Joshua?' Ephraim repeated the name. 'Judah said he was brilliant. He was so proud of him.' He controlled himself with difficulty. There was nothing in his face, but his voice broke. 'I brought something for Joshua from Africa. Seems irrelevant now.'

'It won't be, later,' Henry assured him. 'Benjamin brought him a beautiful gift also, a piece of scripture, original, in a carved wooden box.'

'I brought him a chief's necklace of office, African version of a crown,' Ephraim said. 'It's made of gold and ivory. Symbol of authority. At a glance it seems barbaric, but when you look more closely it's very beautifully carved. Nothing like European at all. I suppose you are right, and in time he will like it. Today it'll seem utterly pointless.'

'That is not all I need to tell you before we get to the house,' Henry went on. They were making quite good speed. The wind had cleared most of the snow off the road. There were one or two places where it had drifted, and they got out and took the spades from the space where the luggage was and helped Wiggins dig a path. Henry saw Ephraim attack the heavy piles with an energy born of anger, his back bent, his weight thrown behind each shovelful. Then they put the spades back and climbed up again to go forward. It was necessary only three times.

'What else?' Ephraim asked without interest when they were on their way again and the broad, white-flecked surface of the lake lay ahead.

'Ashton Gower is out of prison and saying that he was wrongly convicted. The deeds were genuine, and Judah knew it,' Henry answered, pulling the rug a little tighter around both of them. His feet were wet, and the hems of his trousers.

'That's nonsense.' Ephraim dismissed it as of no worth, even to discuss.

'I know it is nonsense,' Henry agreed. 'But he is repeating it very insistently, and Benjamin feels it is important that he is stopped. There are many people in the village

45

who were not there at the time of the trial, and don't know the truth. He is being offensive, and causing Antonia some distress. We cannot ignore him.' He did not add that Benjamin suspected the possibility of his having been involved in Judah's death. Ephraim was not as easy for him to read, and he was uncertain of his anger, or the depth of his pain.

Ephraim did not reply for some time, at least another hundred yards further along the road. Now the white roofs of the village houses were clear in the hard light and the trees were dense black against the grey water.

'Henry, are you saying that there are people who believe him?' he asked at length. 'How could anyone who knew Judah at all consider such a thing even for a moment? There was never a more honest man than he, and Ashton Gower is a vicious cur, without honour, kindness or any other redeeming virtue. Who is there anywhere that can say he has done them a good turn without expecting payment for it?'

'I know it, Ephraim,' Henry replied. 'I think perhaps prison turned his mind. But it doesn't change the fact that he is furious, and bent on clearing his name, whatever the cost.'

'You speak as if you believe he is a danger,' Ephraim said gravely. 'Is he?'

Henry was compelled to admit it. 'I don't know. Benjamin thinks it is possible he had a hand in Judah's death. I cannot discount it either. We met him in the village yesterday, and he has a hatred in him that chilled me. We have told the household servants to be careful locking everything, and to leave the dogs loose at night. It is deeply unpleasant, Ephraim. We can't leave the Lakes, and Antonia and Joshua alone, with this unexplained.' He looked at Ephraim's face, pale under the African sunburn. 'I'm sorry. I wish I could have told you better things.'

Ephraim put his hand on Henry's arm and clasped it hard. 'The truth, Henry. That is all that will serve us. Thank you for coming. We shall need your help.'

Henry did not say that they had it; Ephraim knew that.

It was a quiet, sombre evening, rain and snow alternately beating against the windows and the fire roaring in the hearth. They ate Lakeland mutton and sweet, earth-flavoured potatoes with herbs mixed in. Spices were imported along the coast, and Cumberland gingerbread was famous. Hot, with cream, it made an excellent pudding.

Ephraim and Benjamin spoke quietly together, sharing memories, and Henry sat by the fire with Antonia, mostly listening to whatever she wanted to say, and when she preferred it, telling her tales of London and the busy, city life, which she had never experienced.

Henry slept well, tired after the drive through the wind and snow to Penrith, but he woke early, while it was still dark. He did not wish to lie in bed any longer, and he rose and dressed warmly and was outside before the dawn.

By the time the sun rose over the mountains to the

southwest, and spread soft, pearly light through a mackerel sky, he was more than halfway to the stepping stones at the upper crossing where Judah had died.

Thoughts whirled in his mind as he trudged over the crisp unbroken snow, splashed pink by the sun. Was he imagining the emotion in Ephraim's voice as he asked if Nathaniel's widow were coming as well? Even as he asked himself the question, the certainty of the answer was in his mind: Ephraim himself had been in love with her then, and the memory of it was sharp still.

Of course he would not have seen her since the last time they had both been home, which, as far as Henry knew, was seven years ago. People could change a great deal in such a time. Experience could refine their feelings, or obliterate them.

Henry had not met her, and knew nothing except that she was English, from the east coast, and Nathaniel had known her for only a few months before marrying her. They had left for America shortly after that. Antonia had spoken warmly of her, Judah had seemed to have some reservations, but he had not said what they were. Had they been only an awareness that his youngest brother had loved her as well?

Henry was making his way downhill very slightly now, being careful not to slip. The stream lay ahead of him, running fast. The recent snow had added to it; it washed almost to the top of the stepping stones placed across it, ten in all, flat, carefully chosen.

Where the stream had carved little bays and hollows

out of the bank the current had carried ice down and left it, glittering in the broadening light. The far bank rose more steeply. Henry looked from left to right, but there was nothing except faint indentations where sheep had made tracks for themselves. What on earth would bring Judah here, at night? To be alone with thoughts that troubled him so intensely he could not address them in the house, with Antonia present? Or to meet someone?

Had he been afraid of Ashton Gower and the damage he could cause? Had Gower threatened Antonia, or even Joshua? Would Judah have considered paying him in some way, to protect them?

That was nothing like the man Henry had known. But do people change when those they love are threatened?

He stared up and down the swollen stream. In the daylight he could see the fall clearly, the water splashing white over the jagged rocks. They were certainly sharp enough to have caused the injuries Leighton had described. Everything fitted with the facts. Ice on the stones, one false step, poor balance, even simple tiredness, and a fall could cause a blow that would render one senseless. Face down and one could drown in minutes, the water did not need to be deep. The current could carry a body down to the fall and cause the lacerations Leighton spoke of.

But knowing Gower, why on earth would Judah meet him here, alone at night? The answer was simple. He would not. And to suppose chance made no sense either. Gower would not wait here on a bitter, winter night in case Judah came! That was absurd.

Ashton Gower might well have wished him dead, and rejoice when he was, but there was nothing whatever to suggest that he had killed him, except the madness of the man and his hunger for revenge, and they proved nothing at all.

Reluctantly Henry turned and made his way back, shivering in spite of his coat, scarf, hat and thick, fur-lined gloves. Everything in him wanted to believe Gower was responsible. It was factually absurd, and emotionally the only thing that made sense.

With the daylight the snow was thawing and by the time he reached the house his feet were thoroughly soaked, as were the hems of his trousers. He went up the back stairs to his room and changed before coming down again to the dining room.

Mrs Hardcastle brought him a late breakfast, and he was joined by Benjamin, curious to know where he had been.

'To the stepping stones,' Henry replied when asked. 'Tea?'

Benjamin sat down. He looked tired, his eyes hollowed round with shadows. He accepted the offer Henry poured for them. 'Why?'

'Just to see if what Leighton told us makes sense. It does, Ben. I can't imagine Judah going there to meet Gower at night, and it's ridiculous to think Gower waited there for him by chance.'

Benjamin looked at him steadily. 'You think it was simply an accident?'

Henry did not know how to answer. His intelligence
and his instinct fought against each other. He was a man
used to logical thought, brought up in the discipline and
the beauty of reason. And yet his knowledge of Judah
Dreghorn made the deductions sit ill with him. He
answered the only way honesty could dictate. 'There must
be something we don't know, perhaps several things.'

Benjamin gave a rueful smile. 'Same old Henry, careful
thinker.' He drew in a deep breath and let it out in a sigh.
'We need that now more than ever. What do we tell
Antonia?'

Henry did not have to weigh his answer. There was only
one they could afford, and he had a firmer trust of
Antonia's courage and judgement than Benjamin had,
sharp memories of her frankness, her curiosity and the
courage with which she met the answers, so many of
which she had had to face alone. It hurt him deeply that
her happiness had been so short. 'The truth,' he replied.

The opportunity did not come until the evening. Either
one of them had been otherwise occupied, or Joshua had
been with them, but after dinner they were all gathered
around the fire, and Joshua had gone to bed. It was
Benjamin who began, looking at Antonia with grave
apology.

'I'm sorry to raise it again, but I believe we need to
understand better what happened the night Judah died.'

'I don't know anything I haven't told you,' she
answered, her hands knotted in her lap, unornamented

but for her gold wedding ring.

He was gentle. 'What did you talk about on the way home from the recital?'

'The music, of course.'

'How was Judah? Of course he would be proud of Joshua, but was he otherwise just as usual?'

She considered for a few moments. 'Looking back on it, he was more than usually absorbed in thought. I believed at the time it was the emotion of the music, and that perhaps he was tired. He had had a difficult case in Penrith. I didn't know then just how awful Gower had been. Judah had not told me; I only learned after his death of the details. He's an evil man, Benjamin. To hate so much is a kind of insanity, I think, and that is frightening.'

'Did Judah mention him at all? Can you remember?'

Ephraim sat motionless, his face deep in thought. Henry felt a chill of anxiety. There was a power in Ephraim, a courage that stopped at nothing. If he once were convinced that Ashton Gower had killed his brother, nothing would deter him from pursuing justice. Such strength was disturbing.

'When I think of it,' Antonia replied, 'he actually spoke very little. He only answered me.'

'He didn't say where he was going, or why he wanted to walk at that hour?' Benjamin persisted.

'Not really, just for the air,' she answered. She looked uncertain. 'I thought he wanted to think.'

'Outside, on a winter night?'

She said nothing, now deeply unhappy.

Henry was gentler. 'Did he suggest you should not wait up for him?'

She had to think for a moment. 'Yes. Yes, he did say something like that. I don't remember exactly what.'

'So he expected to be gone an hour or more,' Henry deduced.

'An hour?' Benjamin questioned.

'By the time Joshua had got over his excitement and gone to bed, and then Antonia herself had,' Henry replied. 'It sounds as if he intended to go as far as the stream. What lies beyond it? Where is this Viking site, exactly?'

'Further down the stream,' she said. 'Just above the lower crossing before you get to the church. He wasn't going to the site. There's nothing really beyond the higher crossing, except a copse of trees, and a shepherd's hut. Do you suppose he was going there? What for?'

There was only one answer, and it hung in the air like an additional darkness.

'If it were to meet someone he didn't trust, he'd have taken the dogs. They'd have attacked anyone who threatened him.'

'Or someone he trusted,' Henry said.

Antonia stared at the fire. 'Or there was no one else. He slipped, that's all, just as Dr Leighton said.'

Benjamin's face was bleak. 'Which could not have been caused by Gower. We are no further forward.'

Another thought occurred to Henry. 'Unless he went

with the purpose of helping Gower, perhaps to offer him some kind of assistance in getting himself work, or some establishment in the community again.'

Ephraim's eyes opened wide. 'After what Gower had been saying about him? But if he was, why there, of all places? And in the middle of the night!'

'Judah might have helped him anyway,' Antonia said quietly. 'He helped all kinds of people. But I can't think why meet there!'

'Neither can I,' Benjamin agreed coldly. 'What happened? Gower killed him for his trouble? Or else when Judah slipped, just left him there to drown? I know the man was a swine, but that's inhuman.'

'If he did, we'll prove it,' Ephraim stared at him. 'I'll see him answer for every word, every act. He'll never blacken a Dreghorn name again.'

Antonia smiled and nodded, her eyes brimming with tears.

But alone upstairs in his room, Henry looked out of the window towards the vast, snow-bleached expanse of the mountains under the star-glittered sky, and thought what he had not dared say to the family. He had known Judah well; they had been friends for years, shared all manner of things both with words, and in silence. They had understood the emotions that were too complicated to explain, and talked all night of the philosophies that lent themselves to endless exploration.

He would not have met alone with Ashton Gower to offer him help, after Gower had accused him of fraud, at

54

the stream or anywhere else. He was far too sophisticated not to realise that Gower could then blackmail him with the threat that he had helped only to hide his own guilt, and Gower would do that. That was the kind of man he was, and Judah knew it.

The more he weighed the facts they had, the less any answer fitted them. Each one left loose ends and questions unanswered.

He drew the curtains across and prepared to go to bed. Tomorrow he would have one more journey to make to the station at Penrith, and one more time to break the news.

In the morning the thaw had set in and everything was dripping. Much of the snow had melted and there were long streaks of black over the hills where the slopes were bare. Trees that had been hung with icicles yesterday were naked today, branches an unencumbered lace against the sky.

A grim-faced Mrs Hardcastle served breakfast of eggs, bacon and Cumberland sausage, toast, jam made of witherslacks, or brambles known as black kite, and scalding hot tea in a silver pot. The reason for her anger became known quite early on. Ashton Gower had resumed his accusations and one of the newcomers in the village was repeating it. Mrs Hardcastle's opinion of her should have turned the milk sour.

Henry was ready to set out for the station when Ephraim strode across the stable yard, coat-tails flapping, and climbed in beside him. He offered no explanation and

Henry made no remark. He had a strong idea why Ephraim had come, and he was not sure whether it would make the task of breaking the news to Naomi Dreghorn easier or more difficult. He half expected Ephraim to offer to go in his place, but he did not. It seemed that in this first meeting again after the years between them, and Nathaniel's death, he did not wish to be alone with Naomi.

There was little wind, but the damp in the air made the journey cold. Neither of them had anything further to say about Gower or the subject of his accusations. Henry asked Ephraim about Africa, and was caught up out of the grief of the moment listening to his answers.

Ephraim smiled, and for a space of time he did not see the sweep of snow-scattered hills or the ragged clouds above, but felt the hot sun on his skin and dry winds of Africa carrying the scents of dust and animal dung, eyes narrowed against the light as he saw in his mind's eye the endless plains with vast herds of beasts and the curious flat-topped acacia trees.

'You can hear the lions roar in the night,' he said with a smile. 'It's primeval nature as you never see it in Europe. We've grown old and become too civilised. You hear a hyena's maniacal laughter in the dark, and it's as if you heard the first joke at the beginning of the world, and he's the only one who knows it.'

For a moment Henry also forgot the knife-edge wind with the rain behind it.

'And the plants,' Ephraim went on. 'Every shape and

colour imaginable, and nothing lost or wasted, nothing without a use. It is so superb that sometimes I feel drunk just looking at it.'

They continued to talk.

The time of the journey flew by, and because of the change in the weather, the train pulled in within moments of midday. There were clouds of steam, shouts and a clanging of doors.

Henry did not know Naomi by sight. He realised with surprise that he did not even know what manner of woman to expect. He had been too preoccupied with present events even to form a picture in his mind – tall or short, dark or fair. Now he stood on the platform without any idea at all.

Five women alighted from the train. Two were elderly, and accompanied by men, a third was dark and spare with a grim countenance and severe clothes as if she were applying for a place as a governess in some forbidding establishment. Henry knew Ephraim well enough not even to consider her.

The other two were handsome; the first was fair-haired and dainty, a most feminine woman. She looked about her as if searching for a familiar face.

Henry was about to go forward, certain this must be Naomi, then he saw the other young woman. She was taller, broader of shoulder, and she walked with an extraordinary grace, as if movement were a pleasure to her, an unconsidered and natural art. Her face had an unusual beauty, partly a strength of feature, but even

more an intelligence, as if everything were of interest to
her. If she had ever felt fear, there was no mark of it in
her hearing. Henry could not help wondering if it were
complete innocence, or a most remarkable courage.

He looked sideways, momentarily at Ephraim, and the
last doubt vanished that this was Naomi.

Henry stepped forward. 'Naomi Dreghorn?'

She smiled at him, charming but cool. She did not
know him, and for a moment it seemed that she had not
recognised Ephraim either.

'My name is Henry Rathbone,' he introduced himself. 'I
have come to meet you and take you to the house. You
may remember, it is about six miles away, on the lake.'

'How do you do, Mr Rathbone?' Her smile was wide
and full of pleasure, and she offered him her hand, as if
she had been a man. It was slim and strong, and she
gripped his firmly.

He picked up her case. 'And I expect you remember
Ephraim?'

Her face was calm, but the warmth in it was suddenly
distant.

'Of course. How are you, Ephraim?'

He replied a little stiffly. She might have thought it was
coolness, but Henry could see the uncharacteristic awk-
wardness of his movement; his usual ease, which had its
own kind of grace, was entirely vanished. He was at a
disadvantage that was totally unfamiliar to him.

They spoke of trivialities until they were seated in the
trap and on their way out of Penrith and once again

going westwards, the damp wind in their faces, smelling of rain.

Ephraim asked Naomi about America, sounding as if it were mere courtesy that made him enquire. She replied warmly, with imagination and wit, so that whether he would or not, he was compelled to care. She described the vast plains of the west, the herds of buffalo that made the earth tremble when they ran, the high deserts to which she had travelled from the west, where the earth was red and ochre and the colours of fire, wind eroded to fantastic shapes, like castles and towers of the imagination.

She did not speak of Nathaniel's death, and neither Henry nor Ephraim asked, each waiting for the other to broach the subject of death, and break the news to her. They had half an hour's truce with death while she described travel and adventure, hardship made the best of, and they found themselves laughing.

'I brought a gift for Joshua,' she said with a smile that held a trace of self-mockery. 'I think I chose it because I like it myself rather than because he will, but I didn't mean it to be so. I like to give people things I would keep.'

'What is it?' Henry asked with genuine interest. What would this most unusual woman have brought, to go with Benjamin's scripture in its carved and perfumed case, and Ephraim's king's necklace of ivory and gold?

'An hourglass,' she replied. 'A memento mori, I suppose you would call it. A reminder of death, and the infinite preciousness of life. It is made of crystal and set with semi-precious stones of the desert. The sand that runs through it is red, from the valleys that look like fire.'

'It sounds perfect.' Henry meant it. 'We spend too much of our lives dreaming of the past or the future. There is a sense in which the present is all we have, and we cannot hold it dearly enough. It sounds like a gift of both beauty and memory, like the other gifts he has been brought.'

'You think so?' She seemed to care for his opinion.

If Ephraim was not going to tell her, then he must.

'I do. But before we reach the village, I am afraid there is hard news we have to share.'

'What is it?' She saw that it was serious and the light vanished from her face.

Briefly and in the simplest of words he told her of Judah's death and of Ashton Gower's accusations, including their most recent thoughts and conclusion about them.

She listened very gravely, and spoke only when he had finished, by which time they were less than a mile from the house.

'What are we going to do about it?' she asked, looking first at Henry, then at Ephraim. 'This man must be silenced from slander, and if he is in any way responsible for Judah's death, then we must see that he answers for it! Apart from justice, Antonia and Joshua are not safe unless he is imprisoned again, and his words shown as lies.' There was eagerness and challenge in her face.

This time it was Ephraim who answered. 'We have to prove he was there,' he said grimly. 'It isn't going to be easy because he will have made sure he told no one, and no one else would be out at such a place at night.'

'Why else would Judah go out there in the snow at night, except to meet somebody?' she asked.

There was no answer, and they were approaching the drive gates.

The next hour was taken up in the emotion of arrival and welcome, exchanges of concern, of grief, and of a depth of understanding between the two women, who had both experienced widowhood while still so young. Although they had known each other only briefly, and that several years ago, there was an ease in their communication as if friendship were natural.

They resumed the conversation in the late afternoon over tea by the fire, with scones with hinberry jam, known as raspberries elsewhere, and slices of ginger cake, baked with the spices and rich molasses that came in from the West Indies.

This time Antonia joined in. 'The more I think of it, the more certain I am that he intended to meet someone,' she said gravely. 'I hadn't remembered before, but he took out his pocket watch several times in order to check the time. I thought then that it was to see how long the recital had been, but he would not do that more than once.'

'The difficulty will be to prove that it was Gower,' Benjamin pointed out. 'It is not the easiest place for them to meet, and frankly, a ridiculous time.'

'But Judah was there!' Antonia argued. 'However absurd it is, it is the truth.'

'There is still something we do not know,' Henry insisted. 'Either something important, or that we have misunderstood, and it is not what it seems.'

Ephraim's face set hard. 'Well, two things I am sure of: Judah would not have done anything unjust or dishonest; and the other is that Ashton Gower is a convicted forger, driven by hate and the passion for revenge on the family who legitimately bought his estate. Judah is dead, and Gower is alive and slandering his name.'

'None of that is at issue,' Benjamin agreed. 'The problem is to prove what we believe connects the two.' He turned to Antonia. 'What was Judah wearing that night?'

She looked puzzled. 'It was an evening recital. We were all dressed quite formally.'

'He didn't change before he went out afterwards?'

'No.' She bit her lip. 'I assumed he simply wanted to walk a little after sitting in the hall all evening, and in the carriage on the way back. Why? How can that help?'

'I don't know,' Benjamin admitted. 'But there is no point in trying to find anything on the ground where it happened. All marks or prints will have disappeared long ago. His clothes will have been kept safely. I thought there might be something, a tear, even a note of a meeting, anything at all . . .' he tailed off, losing belief in the hope as he spoke.

'There could be a note,' Henry said, rising to his feet. 'Sometimes things remain dry inside a pocket. If anything at all is legible, it might help. Let us at least look.'

'Of course,' Antonia agreed, standing also. 'I didn't

know what else to do with them. I couldn't bring myself even to clean them . . .' She gave a brief, tight little smile. 'Maybe it is for the best.'

They followed her up the stairs and across the landing to Judah's dressing room. Henry found it disturbing to go into a dead man's private space, see his hairbrushes and collar studs set out on the tallboy, cufflinks in boxes, shoes and boots on their racks. His razor was set beside an empty bowl and ewer in front of the looking-glass in which he must have seen his own face so many times.

He glanced quickly at Benjamin, and saw reflected in his expression exactly the emotions he felt himself – the grief, the slight embarrassment as if they had intruded when Judah was no longer capable of stopping them.

In Antonia Henry saw only the pain of her loneliness. She must have been in here many times before.

Ephraim, several years younger than Judah, carried his loss inside him, concealed as much as he was able. His face was tight, muscles pulling his mouth into a thinner line, eyes avoiding others.

Naomi put her arm around Antonia. She had perhaps done exactly this same grim task, and knew how it felt.

It was left to Henry to go to the top of the chest of drawers where the dark suit was folded, dry and stiff from river water and heavy traces of sand and silt. He opened the jacket and looked at it carefully. It had been little worn, perhaps no more than a year or two old, and made from excellent quality wool. It was beautiful cloth, probably from the fleeces of Lakeland sheep, but the label inside was that of a Liverpool tailor. It told him nothing at all, except the taste of the man who had worn it, which he already knew.

Then he looked in the pockets one by one. He found a handkerchief, stained by water, but still folded, so probably otherwise clean. There were two business cards: a shirt maker in Penrith and a saddler in Kendal. In the wallet there were papers, some of which looked like receipts, but were too smudged to read, a treasury note for five pounds – a lot of money; not that anyone had assumed robbery. The last item was a penknife with a mother-of-pearl handle set with a silver, initialled shield. Presumably any coins would be in his trouser pockets. Henry was about to look when Antonia's voice stopped him.

'What's that?' she said sharply. 'The knife?'

He held it up. 'This? A penknife. He would have one, to sharpen a quill.' It was a very usual thing to carry. He did not understand the strain and disbelief in her face.

'That one!' she exclaimed, holding out her hand.

He passed it to her.

She turned it over, her eyes wide, her skin bleached of colour.

'What is it, Antonia?' Benjamin asked. 'Why does it matter? Isn't it Judah's?'

'Yes.' She looked at each of them in turn. 'He lost it the day before he died.' The words seemed to catch in her throat.

Benjamin frowned. 'Well he must have found it again.

It's easy enough to misplace something so small.'

'Where did he lose it?' Henry asked her.

'That's what I mean,' she stared at him. 'In the stream. He was bending over and it fell out of his pocket. He searched for it, we both did, but we couldn't find it again.'

Ephraim said what Henry was thinking. 'Maybe that's why he went back the night he died.' It was obvious in his face and his voice that he loathed admitting it, but honesty compelled him. 'It's a very nice knife. And it has his initials on it. Perhaps it was a gift, and he cared very much about losing it.'

'I gave it to him,' Antonia said. 'But he didn't lose it at the stones where he was found.' She had to stop a moment to struggle for control of her voice.

There was utter silence in the small dressing room. No one moved. No one asked.

'It was by the bridge a mile and a half further down. The two stones set across the water above it.'

'Further down!' Benjamin was incredulous. 'That doesn't make any sense. It . . .' He did not say it.

Henry knew what they were all thinking. It was in their faces as it was in his mind. Bodies do not wash up stream, only down.

'Are you absolutely certain?' he said quietly.

'Yes.'

It was the proof they needed. Judah had been moved after he was dead, and left where it looked as if he had fallen accidentally.

'Are there any sharp rocks at the lower bridge where he

lost the knife?' Henry pressed.

'No! Just water, deep . . . and gravel.' Antonia closed her eyes. 'He was murdered . . . wasn't he?'

Henry looked at Benjamin, then at Ephraim, then at last back at Antonia.

'Yes. I can think of no other explanation.' He felt stunned by the reality of it. Judah's death had made no sense and they had all been convinced that Ashton Gower was capable of murder. Henry had believed it himself. But it was still different now that it was no longer theoretical but something from which there was no escape.

'What are we going to do?' Naomi asked. 'How do we prove Gower is guilty? Where do we begin?'

Ephraim put his hand up and pushed his hair back slowly off his brow. His eyes were unfocused, staring at something within himself.

Benjamin looked at Antonia, then at Henry. There was horror in his eyes and a deep, painful confusion. Death had hurt him, as he had expected it would, as Nathaniel's death had, but hatred and murder were apart from all he had known. They looked to Henry because he was older, he had an inner calm that concealed his emotions, and he did not betray the pain or the ignorance inside him. He had come to terms with it long ago.

'Tomorrow, when it's light,' he replied. 'We should go to the place where Judah lost the knife, and therefore found it, and see if we can learn anything. We can at least see how long it would take anyone to carry a body from there, upstream to the place he was found, and then go back to the village. If we follow in the steps of whoever did it, we may learn something about them.'

'Yes,' Benjamin agreed. 'That's where we should begin. In the morning.'

They set out together after breakfast. The light was glittering sharp, the lake grey, with silver shadows like strokes from a giant brush. Underfoot the ice crackled with every step; it hung in bright strands from the branches of every tree. The wind drifted ragged clouds, tearing them high, like mares' tails.

They set out walking, Henry and Benjamin ahead, Ephraim alone after them. Antonia and Naomi last, high leather boots keeping their feet dry. No amount of care could keep their skirts from being sodden by the loose snow.

The route to the lower crossing was actually easier. They stood on the bank and stared at the wild, almost colourless landscape. Everything was black rocks, shining water and bleached snow. Of course it would be possible to fall off the stones, but if one did, it would be far from any jagged edges. There were no rocks, no race or fall to cause the injuries Judah had suffered. The bottom of the stream here was pebbles and larger, smooth stones.

'That proves it,' Ephraim said grimly. 'He couldn't have fallen accidentally and hit his head. Someone killed him, and then carried or dragged him upstream to where he was found.' He looked along the bank as he said it, and everyone else's eyes followed his.

'How?' Benjamin asked the obvious question. The ground rose sharply, and a hundred yards away there was a copse of trees straddling both sides. There was no path, not even a sheep track. 'How could anyone carry a grown man's body along there, let alone a big man like Judah?'

'On a horse,' Naomi said quickly. 'That's the only possible way. It's steep, rough and uphill.' She looked at Antonia. 'A horse would leave marks in the snow, at both places. We can't find out now about this place, but Wiggins would remember if there were prints of a horse's hoofs where Judah was found.'

'There was nothing,' Ephraim answered for her. 'I asked, because I wanted to prove that he went there to meet someone.'

'Did it snow any more on the night to fill them in?' Benjamin asked.

'No.' This time it was Antonia who spoke. 'If there were no prints, then there can't have been anyone else there. You can't walk on snow without leaving a mark, whoever you are.' There was pain in her voice, as if a vestige of sense had been snatched from her just when she had thought she understood.

'But he was killed here!' Ephraim insisted. 'Nothing floats up stream!'

'Water,' Henry said aloud.

Ephraim's face tightened, his eyes as cold and blue as the sky. 'Water does not flow upstream, Henry,' he said bitterly. He only just refrained from adding that the remark was stupid and unhelpful, but it was in his expression.

'You can walk in water without leaving a mark,' Henry corrected him. He turned to look up the slope again. 'You could drag a body up the river, walking on the bed and letting the water itself help bear the weight. It's only a mile or so. You'd leave no trace, and it's extremely unlikely anyone would see you. Even if anyone were out, the bed is low-lying naturally, because the stream has cut it. Anything you disturbed would look as if the current did it, and if anyone did come in the light of the half-moon, you would see them black against the snow. And if you bent over, you would simply look like an outcrop of rock, an edge of the bank.'

Benjamin breathed out gently. 'Why didn't I think of that? It's a superb answer. The clever swine! How can we prove it?'

'We can't,' Ephraim bit his lip. 'That's why it's so extremely clever. Sorry, Henry.'

Henry brushed the apology aside with a smile. 'What I don't understand is how Judah lost the penknife the first time, and couldn't find it, yet the second time, in the dark and when he must have had other things on his mind, he saw it!' He looked around at the snow-covered bark, the water clear as glass above the stones, and the dark, roughly cut edges of the stones used for the bridge. They were carefully wedged so they would not slip, even with a man's weight on them.

'Where did he drop it?' Benjamin asked Antonia.

'He bent forward to look at his boot,' she replied. 'He thought he might have cut the leather, but it was only scuffed.'

'And where did you look?'

'On the path, in the snow and at the edge of the water, in case it went in. The mother-of-pearl would have caught the light,' she replied.

Henry looked at the bridge stones where they were wedged. 'Did he put his foot up here to look at the boot?'

'Yes. Oh!' Antonia's face lit. 'You mean it fell between the stones there? And perhaps he remembered . . .'

'Is it possible?' He knew from her expression that it was.

Ephraim turned his face towards the stream. 'Do you suppose Gower took the horse up there, with Judah slung across it?'

They all followed his eyes, seeing the winding course of it, the deeps and shallows.

'Possibly,' Henry answered. 'Or left it here, and walked, dragging him. Neither would be easy, and it would have taken far longer than we originally thought. He must have been away from home a good deal of the night, and half dead with cold after going a mile or more upstream, up to his thighs in icy water, either leading the horse, which would have been reluctant, or dragging the body. And then he had to tramp home through the snow. I wouldn't be surprised if his feet were frostbitten by it.'

'Good!' Ephraim snapped. 'I hope he loses his toes.'

'He wouldn't risk going to Leighton with it,' Benjamin said thoughtfully. The wind was rising, and over to the west the sky was grey. 'There's more snow coming,' he went on. 'We know now what happened. We can make plans what to do best at home. Come on.' And he turned and started to lead the way back again, offering his arm to Antonia.

After having taken off their wet clothes they assembled around the fire. Mrs Hardcastle brought them hot cocoa and ginger cake, then they set about the serious discussion of what they could each do to bring Ashton Gower to justice.

No one questioned that Benjamin had a high intelligence, a keen and orderly mind, which, if he governed the overriding emotion of outrage, he could use to direct the investigation. He could make sense of all they could learn and integrate it into one story to lay before the authorities. His leadership was taken for granted.

Ephraim had courage and a power that would accept no defeat as sufficient to deflect him from his purpose. Now they were certain that there was a crime to solve, his strength would be invaluable.

It was Henry who suggested they should also make use of Naomi's charm to gain what might otherwise be beyond their reach. Laughter and a quick smile often achieved what demand could not, and she agreed immediately, as keen as anyone else to help.

Antonia, newly widowed and with such a young child, was required by custom and decorum to remain at home. Apart from that, she had no desire at all to leave Joshua with a governess or tutor while he puzzled as to what all the adults were doing, and knowing something was desperately wrong but not told what it was, or how they hoped to resolve it. However, her reputation and the regard she had earned in her years in the village would stand well in their favour.

'We will take luncheon early and begin this afternoon,' Benjamin declared. His face was grave as he turned to Ephraim. 'There is at least one man in the village who knows what manner of fellow Gower is, and that is Colgrave. He is not an easy man to like, but he is our best ally in this. Go to him and gain as much of his help as you can. He won't find it hard to believe that Gower could have killed Judah, but don't raise that question unless he does. Remember that we have two objectives: to establish exactly how Judah died.' His mouth pinched tight and his eyes were full of anger. He was finding it hard to control the pain of loss he felt. Judah had been his loved and admired elder brother. His memories were full of laughter, adventure and friendship. To have a creature like Ashton Gower not only end the future but sully the past as well was almost insupportable. 'And to prove it and find justice for him,' he went on. 'But we must also silence his lies for ever and show to everyone that all he says is false. Colgrave might be able to help in both. But be careful how you ask.'

Ephraim's mouth turned down at the corners. 'Don't worry, I shan't trust him,' he replied. 'But he'll help me with everything he can, I promise you.'

Benjamin turned to Naomi. 'Henry and I already spoke to Gower. We met him by chance in the street. He's consumed with hatred. Even death isn't enough to satisfy him. He wants to justify himself and get the estate back for—'

'I'll see him in hell first,' Ephraim said huskily.

'There's no good confronting him,' Benjamin argued. 'We need to determine where he was that night, and if it was even possible for him to have been to the crossing where Judah was killed, and also the stones where he was found. Does he have access to a horse, or did he take one? Did anyone see him, and if so, where and at what time? If we gain anything from him it will be either by charm, or tricking him. Naomi—'

'No!' Ephraim cut across him, instantly protective. 'You can't ask her to speak to him. For God's sake, Ben, he murdered Judah!'

Naomi flushed, seeing the emotion in Ephraim's face.

'He won't know who she is,' Benjamin pointed out, apparently oblivious of it, or of her embarrassment. He could think only of plans. 'And if she went with Henry—'

'I'd rather go alone,' Naomi said quickly. She flashed a smile at Henry, as if he would understand, then looked back at Benjamin. 'To begin with at least, I can pretend anything I wish, or allow him to assume it. If I go with Mr Rathbone, Gower will take against me from the outset, because he knows Mr Rathbone is your friend.'

'He's dangerous,' Ephraim told her, finality in his voice. 'You forget where he's been already. He was eleven years

73

in prison in Carlisle. He's not a . . .'

She looked at him with the shadow of a smile on her mouth, but her eyes were direct, even challenging. Watching them, Henry realised that there was far more than he, or Benjamin, had supposed, and a great deal more emotion.

'We suspect that he murdered a member of our family,' she replied coolly. 'I understand that, Ephraim. I am going to see him openly, and in daylight. He is evil, we are all perfectly certain of that, but he is not stupid. If he were, we would not find him so difficult to catch.'

The dull red of anger spread up Ephraim's cheeks, and a consciousness that he was betraying his emotions too far. It was as if their exchange were not new but merely something in the middle of an established difference.

Benjamin looked at his brother, then at his sister-in-law, aware that he had missed something, but not certain what it was. 'Are you sure you would not prefer to have Henry with you?' he asked.

'Quite sure,' Naomi answered. 'If Gower sees me with anyone from this house we will in a sense have tipped our hands.' She looked at Antonia, and bit her lip. 'Sorry. That is a card-playing expression I have heard men use. I'm afraid I have mixed with some odd company when travelling. Geological sites are not always in the most civilised of places.'

Antonia smiled a smile of genuine amusement for the first time since Henry had arrived, perhaps since Judah's death. 'Please don't apologise. Some time, when this is past, I would like to hear more about it. There are advantages to having a family, but there are chances you lose as well. But I understand the reference. You might be surprised how fierce, and how devious some of the ladies of the village can be about their cards.'

Now it was Naomi who smiled self-consciously. 'Of course, I didn't think of that. The desire to play and to win is universal, I suppose. But believe me, I shall play better against Mr Gower if I do it alone.'

Benjamin conceded. 'I shall go to the village, then follow the path Gower must have taken to see exactly how long it requires, including walking up the bed of the stream.'

'You'll freeze!' Antonia exclaimed with concern.

He smiled at her. 'Probably. But I'll survive. I'll have a hot bath when I get back. I won't be the only man to get soaked through. Shepherds do it regularly. It's time we did something for Judah, apart from talk, and grieve.'

No one argued with him. As he stood up he glanced at Henry. They had not asked him to do anything specific, but the question was in Benjamin's eyes, and Ephraim's as he rose also.

'Oh, I have one or two things to be about,' Henry said, excusing himself as they parted in the hallway.

He went upstairs, changed into heavier clothes, then out to the stables to borrow a horse. He was not willing to tell anyone what he intended. He looked further ahead, and for that he needed to speak to Judah's clerk in his offices in Penrith.

He rode out quickly, hoping not to be seen. He did not

wish to be asked his purpose, not yet.

As he climbed the steep road eastwards, the wind behind him, he turned over the possibilities of the investigation in his mind. What if Benjamin were to discover that it was not practically possible for Gower to have travelled the distance in the time he had? What if Naomi's questions actually proved Gower's innocence, not of intent, but of being able to have committed the act himself? If they failed to prove Gower's guilt, what lay ahead after that? He wanted to find something, a next step to take, other answers to seek. Was there anyone else Gower could have used, willingly or not? Might there have been an ally in the original case, someone who had not come to light then? Did anyone else profit from that tragedy, or from this?

It was a fine horse, and Henry found the ride exhilarating, his mind sharper.

There was always the major possibility that in their loathing of Gower and his appalling accusations, the family had not considered whether Judah had other enemies. He had been a judge for some time. There was little enough crime of any seriousness in the Lakes, but it did exist. He must have sentenced other men to fines or imprisonment.

Who else bore him grudges? Henry did not think for an instant that Judah had been corrupted in anything, but that did not mean that others could not imagine it. Many people refuse to accept that they, or those they love, can be in the wrong, or to blame for their misfortunes. In the short term, it seems easier to blame someone else, to let anger and pride encase you in denial. Some live in it for ever. Some accept their own part only when all vengeance has proved futile in healing the flaw that brought them down. The longer you persist in blaming others, the more difficult it becomes to retreat, until finally your whole edifice of belief rests on the lie, and to dismantle it would be self-destruction.

Who else, apart from Gower, might exist in such a self-made prison? He needed to know, just in case the grief and the anger, the life-long hero worship of an elder brother, had blinded Ephraim and Benjamin to other thoughts.

Henry did not imagine even for an instant that Judah was guilty as Gower accused. He had known Judah well, and loved him as a friend. He had seen him more clearly, having no childhood passions or loyalty of blood. Judah had had faults. He could be overconfident, impatient of those slower of thought than himself. He was omnivorous in his thirst for knowledge, untidy, and he occasionally overshadowed others without realising it. But he was utterly honest, and as quick to see his own mistakes as anyone else's, and never failed to apologise and amend.

Henry needed to know the truth, all of it. They could not defend Judah, or Antonia, with less.

By the time he arrived he knew exactly what he wanted to do. It took him only a few enquiries at the ostler's where he left the horse, before he was sitting in the office of the court clerk, a James Westwood, who received him with grave courtesy. He sat behind a magnificent walnut desk, his spectacles balanced on the end of his rather long nose.

'I can tell you nothing confidential, you understand,' he warned pleasantly.

'Yes, I do understand,' Henry nodded. 'My son is a barrister in London.'

'Rathbone!' Westwood's face lit up. 'Really? Oliver Rathbone? Well, well. So he is your son? Fine man.' He smiled. 'I still can't tell you anything confidential. Not that much of it is, mind you. Nasty business. All very foolish.'

'The estate was in the Gower family?' Henry began. He repeated essentially what Antonia had told him.

'Precisely,' Westwood replied. 'Originally the estate was in the Colgrave family. Then Mariah, the widow of Bartram Colgrave. She married Geoffrey Gower, and had two sons by him. One of them died as a child, the other is Ashton Gower. But the whole thing was much smaller then, before they built that big house, and of course long before they found the archaeological site with all the coins and so on. But I'm ahead of myself.' Westwood coughed and cleared his throat. 'The widow, Mariah Colgrave, brought not only the land, but a great deal of money to her second marriage. With it Geoffrey Gower purchased more land, and built that house that is the centre of the estate now. When he died, it passed to Ashton, his surviving son.'

Henry was puzzled. 'Then what was it that was forged?

And how could Ashton Gower be responsible? It seems to have happened before he was born. How could Peter Colgrave have had any right to it? He wasn't in direct descent.'

Westwood pursed his lips. 'It's not the estate itself, it's the date of it that's at issue,' he explained. 'It all hinges on whether the extra part of it, which includes the house, the better part of the land, and the place where the Viking hoard was found, was purchased before Wilbur Colgrave died, or after.'

'Who was Wilbur Colgrave?' Rathbone was following it with difficulty.

'Bartram's brother, and Peter Colgrave's father. A matter of which way the inheritance went, you see?' Westwood said. 'Before, and it should pass to Peter Colgrave, after and it passes to Mariah, and then to her son, Ashton Gower.'

'Didn't they know that at the time?' Henry still did not understand. 'And if it was a forgery, then Ashton Gower was not even born, so he couldn't possibly be to blame.'

Westwood waved his finger in the air. 'Ah, but it was only questioned when Mariah died, just over eleven years ago. Before that everyone took it for granted.'

'Well, if Mariah forged the deeds, or Geoffrey did, it is still not Ashton Gower's fault!'

'That is the crux of it!' Westwood said, his face sharp with interest in the problem. 'The forgery was recent! They knew that from the ink on the paper, even though whoever did it lifted all the seals off the old one, the

79

family one, and reused them. Very clever, but the rest of it was rubbish!'

'Then why didn't Wilbur Colgrave claim the estate, and the money, at the time? It was rightfully his!' Henry pointed out.

'That is a very good question,' Westwood agreed keenly. 'He is a bit of a scoundrel, and rumour has it that he was always more than a little in love with Mariah – his brother's wife. By all accounts, she was a real beauty in her day. They even said she paid for the land with personal favours.'

He blushed very slightly. 'Least said the soonest mended, I think. Anyway, the part that concerns Judah Dreghorn is that when Ashton Gower came to claim his inheritance, Peter Colgrave swore that the Gower deeds to the estate were forged, and it should be his, as heir to Wilbur Colgrave, who was the younger brother and heir to Bartram, rather than his widow, who forfeited it on remarriage. It was entailed, and supposed to remain in the Colgrave name, except that Wilbur died too, leaving his widow and child, Peter. All rather a mess.'

'And Ashton Gower took advantage to try to prove the estate was his by forging a new deed with the right date for Mariah, and thus for him?'

'Precisely,' Westwood agreed. 'But it failed. The land went back to the Colgrave family, the only one left – Peter. Which was probably where it should have been all the time.'

'And Gower went to prison,' Henry concluded.

'Quite. It was a great deal of money he attempted to steal by fraud,' Westwood said gravely. 'It could not go unpunished. The sentence was perfectly fair and appropriate.'

'So Ashton Gower lost his home and the fortune he had always assumed to be his. No wonder he was bitter.' Henry could imagine it – the young Gower growing up loving the land, riding on it, climbing the hills, feeling he belonged. Then suddenly he lost his father, and his inheritance; the whole nature of his identity and his place in the community was lost too. Little wonder he was so angry he could barely think wisely. But it did not excuse dishonesty, and certainly it was not Judah's fault.

'Why did he blame Judah Dreghorn?' Henry asked.

'Ah!' Westwood steepled his fingers. 'That is something I don't understand,' he admitted. 'Gower completely lost control of himself. He ranted and raved at the Judge, accusing him of corruption, even at the trial. And then afterwards, when Colgrave sold the estate very quickly, and Dreghorn bought it, Gower swore revenge on Dreghorn for having lied about the whole thing. He said the deeds were genuine, and Dreghorn knew it. Which was all patently ridiculous. But it was extremely ugly. Most distressing.'

'And now Judah is dead, in very odd circumstances.' Henry looked steadily at Westwood. 'Do you believe Gower could be so bent on revenge that he would harm him?'

'Oh dear.' Westwood shook his head a little, obviously

distressed. 'You are asking me a highly improper question, Mr Rathbone. It is one I would prefer not to answer. In fact, I really feel that I cannot!' His eyes were very steady, sharp and bright. His refusal was an answer in itself, and he looked at Henry long enough to make sure that he understood it as such.

'I see,' Henry nodded. 'Yes, quite plainly. Do you know why Peter Colgrave did not wish to keep the estate?'

'He is another man about whom I prefer not to express an opinion.' He smiled very slightly and stared at Henry over the tops of his spectacles. 'Don't press me into something which would be indiscreet, and might embarrass us both.'

Henry gave a half-smile. 'Thank you. At least I think I understand something of the actual issues, but not why Ashton Gower imagined he could get away with anything so stupid.'

'Arrogance,' Westwood said quietly. 'I imagine he made the forgery in the heat of anger, perhaps when he discovered the original and realised what it would mean to him. Then he could not back out of it. But that is only my guess.'

Henry thanked him and went outside into the cold, already darkening afternoon.

They met before dinner, a little later than usual. Mrs Hardcastle had prepared a magnificent meal, and the whole house was decorated for Christmas with wreaths of holly, ivy and pine. There were polished apples of red, yellow and green, and baskets of nuts tied with gold ribbons.

Henry saw it with surprise, in view of the recent, terrible bereavement, and glanced uncertainly at Antonia, in case the servants should have done it without her permission.

She smiled back at him. 'It's still Christmas,' she said very quietly. 'We must not forget or ignore that. Without Christmas, there would be no hope. And I have to have hope: wild, unreasonable, against all the logic that man can have, things only God can do.'

'We all have to,' he agreed as they walked into the dining room side by side. 'We'll definitely keep Christmas. Thank you.'

They took their places and the dishes were served one after another. They were ready for pudding when they finally approached the subject of their achievements during the day.

'I walked the distances,' Benjamin said thoughtfully. 'It's possible to cover them all between the time Judah could have got to the stream and the time his body was discovered, but only if you don't hesitate. And there would be no time for Gower to have waited for Judah more than five minutes. Not if Judah went straight there. Of course, he could have waited for Gower, because we have no idea when he died, except that it was some time before three o'clock when they found him. Also we don't know what time Gower got home again.' He turned to Naomi. 'Perhaps you do? Did you manage to see him?'

Naomi gave a rueful little shrug. 'It was easier than I expected.' She looked at Benjamin, avoiding Ephraim's eyes, but he clearly knew she was perfectly aware that he was looking at her.

'How did you do it?' Antonia asked.

Naomi smiled at her. 'With more invention than I am proud to admit,' she answered. 'Let me do you the favour of not telling you, so you can meet the village with complete innocence. People speak of you so highly.' She looked at Antonia with candid regard. 'You are much admired, even by those who are stupid enough to listen to Gower. Your reputation is your greatest asset. And when we all go away again, you will remain here and it will matter that it is not changed.'

Antonia smiled, but she did not attempt to speak.

Henry had not thought of it in quite those bold terms before, and he realised that perhaps Antonia had not either. None of them had looked beyond the shock and anger of the present. But, of course, Benjamin would return to the Holy Land. He was probably in the middle of some great excavation. Ephraim would go back again to Africa and his exploration, the plants and discoveries that so fascinated him. Naomi would make the long journey back to America, and then westwards once more to take up Nathaniel's work, and her own friends in the life they had made there. Even Henry would return to Primrose Hill, and the joys and cares of London. Antonia would then taste the full measure of her loneliness.

Henry remembered the death of his own wife. At first

shock numbs much of the deepest ache. There are things that have to be done, people told, arrangements made. One forces courage to surmount weakness and for the sake of other people, one behaves with dignity.

But afterwards, when the first mourning is over and the attention goes, friends and family return to their own lives, then the true weight of loss descends. Everything one used to share is no longer as it was. The silence of the heart is deafening. Antonia had yet to face that.

Naomi had already experienced it, but she at least had some work that would occupy her energies and her thoughts. Of course Antonia had the estate to run, and her care for Joshua, but his grief was her burden as well.

'What did you learn?' Benjamin was asking Naomi now. She had already answered some of his questions, and Henry had not been listening.

'Gower seems to have spent the evening with the Pilkingtons,' Naomi replied, a faint look of distaste on her face. 'Mrs Pilkington is a woman of extraordinarily generous bosom, balanced by an opposingly mean spirit. She has opinions as to the moral value of everything, good or bad. "Decadent" is her favourite word. I don't know why, because I don't think she knows what it means.'

'She is new money?' Henry enquired, aware of all the social differences that carried, the envy and the ambition.

Naomi's face lit with a smile, broad and candid. 'Exactly! Old money must be immorally obtained. Hers is new, of course. She has espoused Gower's cause, precisely because the older families can't stand him. And the violin recital was "decadent", so she did not attend. She probably doesn't know Bach from Mozart, and doesn't want to be upstaged, poor soul.' There was a sudden thread of pity in her voice, as if the absurdity of pretension had betrayed its inner fear and its emptiness.

Ephraim saw it, and a shred of its meaning registered as surprise on his face, not at the village, but at what he had glimpsed in Naomi, a new beauty. 'But Gower was there?' he grasped at the personal meaning.

'Yes. He left to go home at just after ten,' she replied.

'Then he could have got to the lower crossing by the time Judah did,' Benjamin deduced. 'But it would have been hard. Don't the Pilkingtons live right down by the water?'

'Yes.'

He thought for a moment. 'He would have to have had luck on his side,' he said. 'Or else Judah stood around for some time waiting for him. I asked everyone I could about that day, the servants here, in the post office and in the village. There's no word of anyone delivering a message to Judah to meet Gower, or one from Judah to him. And it's not a place anyone would meet by chance.'

'Frankly, it's not a place anyone would meet at all,' Henry said. 'I still find it hard to accept.'

'We have to,' Benjamin argued. 'That's where Judah was, or he couldn't have found the knife. And the higher crossing is just as absurd, but that's where he was found.' He turned to Naomi. 'What did you think of Gower?'

She hesitated. 'A very angry man, one who hits out first, in case he doesn't get a later chance,' she replied. 'A man so filled with his own emotions he doesn't have time or room to consider anyone else's. I'm not sure that I wanted to see any good in him, but if there was any, it was easy to overlook. But he is far from a fool. Which is why I wonder how he ever thought he could get away with such a stupid forgery.'

'Even the most intelligent people can behave idiotically once in a while when their passions are in control,' Henry said, pursing his lips as memory stabbed him. 'We lose peripheral vision and see only what we want. It's a sort of mental arrogance. Being intelligent is not always the same thing as being wise – or honest.'

Naomi looked at him and the warmth of her smile was as if the fire had suddenly burned up, dispelling the shadows and the cold places in the room.

'No, it isn't,' she agreed. 'But they are the things most worth winning, and without them the rest is of little value. I should be more sorry for Ashton Gower, and for stupid Mrs Pilkington. It's themselves they are cheating in the end.'

Ephraim sat very quiet, almost without moving. One needed to look at him carefully to realise how fully his concentration was on Naomi.

'Could he have killed Judah? Is it possible?' Benjamin asked softly.

Ephraim turned to him. 'Yes,' he answered. 'And I can't like Colgrave, he's a cold man, for all that he hides it, but he'll help us, at least in this. He hates the injustice, for us and for the whole village. It's bad for everyone.'

Benjamin nodded. 'Good. We have made a start, but it is not proof.'

'What else can we do?' Antonia asked. She was troubled, trying hard to hide the desperation inside her. She was beginning to face the long future ahead after they had gone and she was alone in the village – the whispers, the thoughts, her dead husband's memory to protect and her son to nurture, and keep his faith and certainty strong.

Benjamin looked at her. 'I don't know yet. But we will succeed. Judah was our brother, and I, at least, will never leave here until I have cleared his name, I promise!'

'Nor will I,' Ephraim said fiercely. 'I give you my word, for you, for Joshua, and for Judah himself.'

She bent her head, the tears spilling over her cheeks. 'Thank you.'

The morning was sharp with high, drifting clouds and a thin sunshine. Henry rose early, had a cup of tea, and then dressed and went out. He preferred to walk alone and think. They had spoken brave words the evening before, but they had no plans that were assured of giving them the proof they needed. They were loyal, that was never in question. They were brave. Benjamin had the logic and the acute intelligence to marshal all the information they could acquire, and the force of mind to present it. Ephraim had the strength to face whatever unpleasantness, difficulty or obstruction the people in the village might use, or to face Ashton Gower himself. Nothing would cause him to retreat from what he believed to be right, no matter what the cost.

And Naomi had a charm and wit, an imagination to understand others, a warmth to disarm them, so she could glean all kinds of information that a more direct, confrontational approach would not. Henry found himself liking her more with each encounter. He could easily see why Ephraim had fallen in love with her, and remained so even over the years since she had left. In fact it was less easy to understand why Benjamin had not!

Why had she chosen the quieter, far less dynamic Nathaniel? That was something Henry felt he would never understand. But then what man ever really understands the choices of women?

He walked rapidly westwards along the way Judah had gone on the night of his death. Apparently it was the easiest way from the house to the site of the Viking hoard, and he had not yet seen it. The air was crisp and sweet, and he saw birds wheeling in the sky and only a little higher on the slopes of the hills, the dark forms of deer grazing. A winter-coated hare loped across the snow only twenty yards away. He thought how infinitely more beautiful this was than the dripping, smoke-darkened streets of London, or of any other city.

He crossed the stream over the narrow stone bridge, balancing with great care, although there was not actually ice on it, as he was much relieved to find.

Then instead of going towards the church, he turned

upstream and followed the path where it had led along the bank, and then climbed away. There was a small wooden notice indicating that he was almost there.

He saw it as soon as he breasted the rise, its remaining walls etched dark against the snow. Behind it a lone man stood staring across the wind-rippled water, which was blue and silver and grey. Henry knew who it was before his footsteps crunching on the snow made the man turn: Ashton Gower, bare-headed, his black hair and fierce eyes making him look as if he belonged to the land-scape, even to the period when this shrine had been built. It gave Henry an odd feeling of intrusion, as if he were trying to alter history to make his own people belong in someone else's heritage. He dismissed the thought with irritation. It was a trick of the light and his imagination.

'Good morning, Mr Gower,' he said politely. He con-sidered saying something agreeable about the view, or even the possibility of more snow blowing up from beyond Helvellyn, and changed his mind. It would make him sound as if he were nervous. He did not mean it, and they both knew that.

Gower swept his arm wide. 'Like it?' he asked. 'I'd welcome you to my land, but the law has taken it from me. You can come here any time you want, if the Dreghorns say you can. I can come here only to the point open to the public. But I refuse to pay!'

'Has anyone asked you to?' Henry enquired, standing beside him and looking at the water, the mountains and the sky – wild, wind-ragged, the ever shifting patterns of light and shadow.

'Not yet,' Gower replied. 'Even Dreghorn hadn't the nerve to do that. He knew he was wrong, you know. He couldn't look me in the eye. More grace than his brothers.' His mouth twisted. 'Or more guilt!'

'I've known Judah Dreghorn for twenty years,' Henry told him levelly, controlling his temper with difficulty. 'Apart from what I know, there's no one else who has an ill word to say of him. I also know what they say of you, Mr Gower, and it is far less flattering. I assume you are claiming that the experts in forgery were all lying as well? Why? Are you so hated here that men will perjure their souls to see you punished for something you did not do? Why? What have you done to earn that?'

Gower shivered, hunching his shoulders as if the wind were suddenly blowing off ice. 'The deeds I got from my father's safe were genuine,' he said, facing Henry directly. 'I can't prove that, but they were. The land was his. Wilbur Colgrave might have been in love with my mother, but no Colgrave yielded his land for anyone. The reason he didn't claim it was that he had no right to. That whole story of an affair was a slander. But who can prove that now?' There was pain in his voice, deep and angry, but so real Henry could feel it tear inside him also. Perhaps it was for his mother's reputation as much as for himself. Henry would find it unbearable, were such a thing suggested of his mother.

How much can pain justify? Did Colgrave have to have

revealed that very private detail? Could he not at least have kept that much silent? There was an unspoken understanding that one did not blacken the names of the dead who could no longer speak for themselves!

But then that was exactly what Gower was doing to Judah. Henry said as much aloud.

Gower turned to stare at him, confusion and frustration in his face. 'How else can I defend myself?' he demanded, his voice almost choking. 'This land is mine! They took my home, my heritage, my mother's good name, and mine! And made me pay for it with eleven years of my life, while they took the spoils. Now I'm a branded man, without a roof over my head except I labour for it, and pay week by week. I'm supposed to accept that? That's your idea of justice, the Dreghorn way?'

'And the forged deeds?' Henry asked. 'Or did all the experts lie? Why? Is Judah Dreghorn supposed to have paid them too?'

'I don't know. I do know the document I gave them was genuine, and it said the land was my father's. The dates were right.' There was no doubt in Gower's face, no flicker, only blind, furious certainty.

There was no answer. Henry turned away and walked back to the house. He went straight to the stable, requested a horse, and rode out along the road to Penrith. He needed to know the exact history of where the deeds had been kept from the time of Geoffrey Gower's death until the expert from Kendal had examined them and pronounced them to be forged. Doubt was gnawing at his mind, shapeless, uncertain, but fraying the edges of all his thoughts. He did not doubt Judah's honesty, but could he have been mistaken, perhaps duped by someone else? It was a disturbing idea, but Henry could not leave it unanswered.

The town was busy with the usual trade and market. The streets were crowded with people coming and going. Wagons were piled with bales of woollen cloth. All the traditional manufactures of the Lakes were there: clogs, slate, bobbins, iron goods, pottery, pencils, and every kind of food, oats, mutton, fresh fish, especially salmon, potatoes, Forty Shilling and Keswick Codling apples, and spices from the coast.

Henry pushed his way through and eventually found himself at Judah's offices again. It was a long, tedious task to trace the arrival of the deed and its exact whereabouts from that time forward until it was taken to show the specialist in Kendal.

'Ah, yes,' the junior clerk said knowingly. 'Very sad. Never suspected Mr Dreghorn of anything like that, I must say. Goes to show.'

Henry froze, anger boiling up inside him. 'Goes to show what, Mr Johnson?' he said coldly. 'That memories are short and loyalty thin?' Then the instant he had said it he regretted his lack of self-control. He was making his own task harder.

Johnson flushed scarlet. 'I don't believe them!' he protested. 'You do me wrong to think I did, sir, and that's a fact.'

Henry shifted his own position, perhaps a little less than honestly. He had assumed the man was speaking for himself. There had been no outrage in his face. 'I was referring to those who do, whoever they are,' he amended. 'I trust that having known Mr Dreghorn you would be the last to agree, and the first to defend him.'

'Of course I would,' Johnson said with a sniff.

Henry used his advantage. 'Then I am sure you will be as eager as I am to clear it up beyond question. I need to follow the history of those deeds that were sworn to be forgeries. When did they come here? Who brought them and from where? Where were they kept? Who had access to them, and who took them to Kendal to show to . . . what is his name?'

'Mr Percival, sir.'

'Yes. Good. If anyone did tamper with them, it was not Mr Dreghorn.' He made it a statement that could not be argued with.

'Of course it wasn't!' Johnson agreed truculently.

But it was a slower task than Henry had expected, and Johnson was, above all, protective of his own reputation. He now had a new master and was determined to appear in the right. Judah was gone and could be of no more help.

Henry caught him in a couple of self-serving lies before he was certain beyond argument as to the history of the deeds. The matter had taken well over a week, and during that time no one had looked at them. Undeniably, Judah could have altered them, or replaced them with forgeries.

But so could a number of other people with either access to the office, or to the messenger who had carried them to Kendal. And, of course, it still left the time they had been in Mr Percival's care, a further two weeks or more. All were unlikely, but none was impossible.

Henry thanked Johnson, who was now a good deal more anxious, then returned to the stable where he had left his horse, and set out on the long ride back to the estate.

He turned the problem over in his mind all the way. Who had had the time, the opportunity and the skill to make the forgery? The paper had apparently been wrong, and the ink, so they were easy enough to come by. The old seals had been removed from the original deeds, and glued back on the new ones. Time seemed to be the major element. But they had been in Judah's offices for a week, then transported to Kendal and in Percival's office for a further two weeks. For anyone familiar with the deeds it would take only a day to take them, create the forgery, destroy the original, and put the forgery back.

It might be more difficult to prove who had actually done it. Unfortunately Judah was the person with the best opportunity – apart from Mr Percival, of course. But there was no reason to suppose he had any interest in the matter.

Henry continued to think about it as he rode. He found the stark beauty of the winter landscape peculiarly comforting. Its clean lines, wind-scoured, had a kind of courage about them, as if they had endured all that the violence of nature could heap on them, and pretension was swept away. The cold air stung his face, but his horse was a willing and agreeable animal, and there was a companionship in their journey. He thanked it with affection when he finally dismounted in the stable yard and went into the house.

The evening was much more difficult. No one else had learned anything they felt to be of use. The whispers in the village were growing louder and each of them had heard remarks that at the best could be regarded as doubting, beginning to question whether Judah was actually as honest as he had seemed. Other cases were recalled where people had protested their innocence, even though a jury had found them guilty. There was no direct accusation, nothing specific to deny or disprove, just an unpleasantness in the air.

Henry said that he had been to Penrith. He did not want to make a secret of it or it might seem underhand, and, anyway, the groom would know because of the horse. But he did not tell anyone why he had gone, or precisely where.

They sat around the dinner table with another delicious meal. Mrs Hardcastle had made one of the local delicacies for pudding – a dish known as Rum Nicky – made of rum, brown sugar, dried fruit and Cumberland apples.

Antonia spoke because it was her home and they were her guests. She would not allow them to sit uncomfortably in silence, but it was all trivia, little bits of news about sheepdog trials last summer, boat races on the lake, who had climbed which mountain, what weather to expect.

Henry was aware of Ephraim one moment looking at Naomi, the next carefully avoiding her eyes. Whatever it was that he felt for her, she did not wish to acknowledge it, and yet Henry was absolutely certain that she knew.

And all the time at the back of his mind was the fear that they would all have to be told the possibility that in some way, through misplaced trust, inattention, some kind of carelessness, Judah had made an error, and Gower was not guilty of forging the deeds, which must mean that someone else had.

Who else had profited? Peter Colgrave, that was obvious. Had anyone else thought they could buy the estate cheaply? Had anyone known of the Viking hoard, with its gold and silver coins, its jewellery and artefacts, not to mention its historic value? That was another thing to find out, if possible.

But sitting at the table, seeing their faces, the tension, the anger and the grief, Henry dared not approach it yet. But how long could he wait?

After the meal was finished Antonia went upstairs to say good night to Joshua, and Henry knew from the evenings before that she would be gone for quite a long time, perhaps an hour or more. Joshua was nine years old, still a child in his hurt and confusion, trying hard to earn the respect of his uncles, to behave like the man he thought they expected him to be.

And he was also intelligent enough to know that they were protecting him from something else. Henry had seen his face as they changed the subject when he came in while they were speaking of Gower, or the village. They did not know children. They did not realise how much he heard, how quick he was to catch an evasion, a note of unintended patronage. He could see fear, even if he could not give it a name.

Henry could remember how Oliver had constantly surprised him with his grasp of things Henry had assumed to be beyond him. He watched, he copied, he understood. Joshua Dreghorn was just as eager and as quick. Antonia knew that, and she was spending her time, and perhaps her emotions, with him.

Henry invited Naomi to accompany him for a short walk in the starlit garden, which she accepted. He held her cloak for her, then put on his own coat, and led the way to the side door.

'What is it?' she asked as soon as they were a couple of yards from the house. 'Have you learned something?'

There was no time to approach it obliquely. 'I went to see a clerk in Judah's office in Penrith,' he answered. 'I asked him exactly where the deeds had been since they were taken out of Geoffrey Gower's safe.' He spoke quietly, although the crunch of their footsteps on the frost-hardened grass might well have disguised their voices, had anyone near an open window been listening. 'There was time and opportunity for someone to have altered it . . . changed it for another.'

'You mean put a forgery in place of a genuine one?' she saw what he meant immediately, and there was fear in her

98

voice. With the hood of her cloak up he could see little of her face.

'Yes,' he replied.

'You believe Gower?' It was a direct question, filled with incredulity, but asked none the less.

He could not answer immediately, not with complete honesty.

'Mr Rathbone?' she demanded, gripping his arm and pulling him to a stop.

'I don't believe Judah would have done such a thing, for any reason whatever,' he said unhesitatingly. Of that he was absolutely sure. 'But he may have trusted people he should not have.'

Her voice was very low. 'Have you told that to anyone else?'

'No.' He was smiling in the dark, but it was self-mockery; there was no pleasure in it at all. 'I have spent all my ride back from Penrith, and a good deal of the evening trying not to do so. But it is a possibility we have to face.'

'You are sure there was opportunity?'

'Yes.'

'Who? If not Gower, why would anyone else? He was the only one who would profit from such a stupid forgery!'

They started to walk again, heading further away from the house, and anyone who might look out and see them.

'He made the date into the one that would mean the property was his!' she went on, still holding his arm. 'The

99

other date would have left it as Peter Colgrave's, as it was. Then we bought it. No one else had anything to gain from changing it.'

'There is no answer that fits the facts,' he told her. 'Ashton Gower swears that the deeds were not forged, the experts say that they were. The forged date favours Gower.'

'Yes. Isn't that proof?'

The thought he had been fighting against all day crystallised in his mind.

'What if the forgery is not a change at all?'

'But that makes no . . .' she stopped. 'Oh, no! You mean if the forgery is an exact copy of the original, date included? So Gower was telling the truth when he said the deed was genuine? Then it was replaced by an obvious forgery, with exactly the same date, so Gower would be disbelieved – lose his land!'

'Yes.'

'That is terrible! But who? Colgrave?'

'Perhaps. Or anyone else who thought they might be able to buy the estate cheaply.'

'Judah bought it from Colgrave, at the price he asked. He was in a hurry for the money. I think he had debts. Maybe someone else expected to buy, and didn't get the chance. That could be anyone!'

'Maybe someone else had already found the Viking hoard and knew what it would be worth,' Henry pointed out. 'Colgrave didn't, or he would have asked a far larger sum.'

'And Gower believes it was Judah.' Her voice was sombre and tight with strain. 'Perhaps he really didn't do it – is that possible? Without knowing it, Judah sent an innocent man to prison!'

'Yes, it is possible.' He loathed admitting it. 'Of course, it is also possible that he is as guilty as sin of killing Judah,' he added. 'Somebody did. No one else we know had a reason – except the real forger.'

'Perhaps Gower has enemies too?' Naomi suggested. 'He's a most disagreeable man. Is it possible he is the real intended victim, and Judah is only the means they use?'

'Yes, of course it is. And I don't know where we would even begin to look for them!'

She bent her head. 'This is terrible!' she said in a whisper. 'We have to know! Don't we?'

'I think so. Could you rest with it unanswered?'

'I don't know. It doesn't matter for me. When it's over, when we've silenced Gower, I'll go back to America again. I love the excitement, the discovery, the sheer blazing beauty of it. There is a magic to the unknown like nothing else.' Her voice was filled with vitality.

It reminded Henry of Ephraim when he had spoken of Africa and the wild, marvellous beauty of that country too. Again he wondered why Naomi had chosen the safer Nathaniel, with his softer ways?

'Do you miss it?' he asked aloud.

'I've been too busy to, so far,' she said honestly.

'We will have to tell the family the possibilities that the deeds were changed,' he said as they came to the end of the lawn and looked across at the glimmering light on the lake, visible only as movement, like black silk in the wind.

'I know. Antonia will be terribly hurt, as if we have suddenly abandoned her.' She sighed. 'Benjamin will be confused, but I think he can't be utterly shocked. He's too clever not to have thought of it, even if only to deny it.'

'And Ephraim?' he asked, knowing she would find that hard to answer.

She hesitated before she spoke. 'He'll be angry. He'll think we have betrayed Judah. He doesn't forgive easily.'

Henry looked at her, the little of her face he could see in the starlight, but all he could glean from her was the emotion he heard in her voice. Was it in general she thought Ephraim did not forgive, or was there some specific sin she spoke of? Had Nathaniel really been her first choice, or was he second, and she would not now make a decision, even for her own happiness, which she felt betrayed him? She had used the word herself, referring to Ephraim's emotions.

He asked, even though it was intrusive. 'You speak as if you know him well, and I can't help seeing his feelings for you.'

She smiled. 'You are wondering why I married Nathaniel, when Ephraim also asked me?'

'Yes,' he admitted.

'Because love is more than passion and excitement, Mr Rathbone. If you trust your life and your love to someone, you need to admire their courage, and Ephraim has any amount of that. But if you are going to live with them every day, not just the good ones, but the bad ones as well, the difficult ones when you fail, make mistakes, feel bruised and afraid, you need to be certain of their kindness. You need someone who will forgive you when you are wrong, because you will be wrong sometimes.'

He did not interrupt. They stood side by side, looking towards the water. It was cold and very clear, the stars tiny, glittering shards of light in the enormity of space.

'Ephraim has not been wrong often enough to understand,' she said almost under her breath.

'It seems to me you are not wrong very often either,' he observed. 'And yet you have a gentleness.'

This time he saw her smile. 'I have been. I look like my mother. She behaved badly. I never knew why, but I imagine sometimes how lonely she might have felt, or what made her do as she did. My father never forgave her for it, so even if she had wished to return her heart to him, he did not allow her to.'

Henry pictured another woman like Naomi, perhaps bored, with nothing on which to use her intelligence, no adventure to take her from the domestic round, and possibly loved more for her beauty than for her inner self. How deeply had her unhappiness marked her daughter that she chose the gentleness of a forgiving man rather than the passion of one she feared might repeat her mother's history?

'I see,' he said very gently. 'Of course you did. We all need to be forgiven, one time or another. And we need to talk, to share our own dreams, as well as those of the one we love.'

She reached up very gently and kissed his cheek. 'I always liked Nathaniel, and I learned to love him. I loved Ephraim from the beginning, but I don't trust him to forgive my mistakes, and forget them, and to hold my heart softly.'

For a moment or two he did not speak. When he did it was of the problem they shared, now a burden growing heavier by the minute.

'I think I shall go to Kendal tomorrow and see these experts who testified about the deeds.' He turned to face her. 'Then I have to tell Benjamin and Ephraim what I find, and I suppose, if it is irrefutable, Antonia too.'

'Do you think Ashton Gower was imprisoned falsely?' she asked.

'I think that it is possible, and if it is true, then we must acknowledge it and try to redress as much of the injustice as may be reached now.'

'But somebody killed Judah!' she protested. 'His body did not wash upstream! And if Gower really was innocent, does that not give him the most intense reason to seek revenge? Perhaps he didn't mean to kill Judah, it was just a fight that ended when Judah slipped and fell, and for some reason Gower dragged his body all the way up to the higher crossing. But why would he do that?'

'Maybe at the time of Judah's death there were some signs in the snow that another person had been there, and even of the struggle,' Henry reasoned. 'He could not afford to have it investigated, or at that time it might have been easy enough to show he was there too. And with their history, who would believe him that it was accidental?'

'I think he is a loathsome man,' she said, beginning to walk slowly back towards the house. 'But I am sorry for him. If it really was an accident, then if we could help him prove it, we ought to – oughtn't we?'

'Yes.' He had no doubt.

'The family won't like that.' There was certainty in her voice too, and fear. She wanted to belong. She had loved them all since she had first known them. They were the only family she had. Like Antonia, she was otherwise alone.

'We don't know yet,' he pointed out. 'At least not beyond doubt. I'll go to Kendal tomorrow.'

And with that they walked back up the grass and in through the door again to the warmth.

In the morning Henry rode early to Penrith, and took the train to Kendal, which was the next stop on the way south towards Lancaster. He was in the town by half-past ten, and found the office of the expert in forged documents, Mr Percival. He was younger than Henry had expected, perhaps no more than in his middle thirties. He was clean-shaven, with a thick head of reddish-brown hair, and an agreeable expression as he showed Henry into his office.

The pleasure in his face faded rather rapidly when

Henry explained the area of his interest.

'Yes, I heard that Gower was making accusations,' Percival said drily. 'A great shame. A most unpleasant man, and completely irresponsible. A tragedy that Dreghorn should die in a wretched accident like that. However, I don't see that there is anything I can do to assist you, Mr Rathbone.' He leaned back a little with a slight smile. 'You need a solicitor. Such slanderous talk should be addressed by the law. I am sure Mrs Dreghorn already has someone who represents the family, but if you need anyone further, I can recommend someone easily enough.'

'Thank you, but that is not necessary.' Henry reminded himself that this man was a forgery expert, a witness in court, but not a lawyer of any kind. Nothing that he said to him was he obliged to keep in confidence. 'I am interested in learning more of precisely what happened. I think that is a far better defence than legal restriction, and certainly swifter and more honest than suits for slander, which may drag on and become most unpleasant.'

Percival leaned back in his chair and bit his lower lip. 'The truth, Mr Rathbone, is that the deeds to the estate owned by Geoffrey Gower and bequeathed to his son, Ashton Gower, were actually forgeries, and not very good ones. That has been established at law, and Ashton Gower sentenced to prison for his part in it.'

'How do we know that it was Ashton Gower who forged them, and not his father?' Henry asked with an air of innocence.

Percival smiled patiently. 'Because in earlier sight of them, during previous transactions, they were never questioned. And frankly, Mr Rathbone, the forgeries were extremely poor. No one used to dealing in legal documents of any sort would have been fooled by them.'

'And yet you did not immediately report the fact that they were forged,' Henry pointed out. 'At first glance, you noticed nothing amiss.'

Percival coloured uncomfortably. 'I looked only at certain parts of them, Mr Rathbone, I confess to that. The first reading of them in their entirety showed us the falsity of them. There is no question. Frankly, I am not sure what it is you are trying to prove. Gower is a forger. Judah Dreghorn had no choice but to sentence him to imprisonment. Everything else is spurious, just a weak and vicious man making excuses for himself.'

'You have a deep personal dislike for Gower, Mr Percival,' Henry observed.

Percival's face tightened. 'I do. And I am far from alone, Mr Rathbone. He is a most objectionable man, without the grace or the honesty to repent of his crime, nor the courage to begin again and attempt to live a decent life. Instead of that, which might earn him forgiveness, he has attempted to blacken the name of an honest judge who did no more than his duty. If you had known Judah Dreghorn, you would understand my anger.'

'I did know him,' Henry said, keeping his voice calm only with an effort. 'He was my friend for over twenty years. Mrs Dreghorn is my goddaughter. That does not address the question of who forged the document, and when.'

'For heaven's sake, man!' Percival snapped. 'Ashton Gower forged it at some point between the original being taken from his father's safe, and this forgery produced to justify his claim to the estate!' Percival snapped.

'You are an expert in forgery?'

'I am!'

'So it would be brought to you for that purpose, but not until forgery was suspected?'

'Of course.'

'Who saw it first, prior to that?'

'William Overton, a solicitor.'

'Did he testify in the case?' Henry asked.

'No.'

'Why not?'

'He was not called. Why should he be? No one claimed that the deeds were genuine, except Gower himself, and he was obviously lying. As I said, Mr Rathbone, the work was shoddy to a degree. Any examination of them made the fact plain. Now, if you don't mind, I have other clients to see, to whom I may be of more service. I am afraid I cannot help you, and to be candid, I have no desire to. You seem to be defending a man who has maligned a judge we all admired, and who apparently considered you to be a friend.'

Henry remained sitting. 'When is it supposed that Gower forged the deeds, Mr Percival?'

Percival was barely patient. 'Before he brought them to his solicitor, sir! When else?'

'Mr Overton?'

'Precisely.'

'They passed from him to Mr Overton, to you?'

Percival hesitated, his face a trifle flushed. 'No, not exactly. They were questioned by Colgrave, and he demanded sight of them, which happened in Judge Dreghorn's office, I believe.'

'Why not in Mr Overton's? Was he not the Gowers' solicitor?'

'Mr Colgrave required that it be before a judge, and Mr Overton was perfectly satisfied that it be so. I really don't understand what it is you are trying to prove, Mr Rathbone!' Percival said irritably.

'I am trying to see when they might have been tampered with, that Mr Gower could sustain an accusation that Judah Dreghorn, or anyone but himself, could have forged them,' Henry replied.

'For heaven's sake, man! You don't believe him!' Percival was aghast.

'I am trying to prove Judah Dreghorn's innocence,' Henry answered. 'If he never had them in his possession, then he must be!'

'Well . . . well, his reputation is sufficient. The deeds were in several different people's possession, if you wish to be legal about it. It would be far better, and wiser, if you were to allow the matter to drop. No one will believe Gower. The man is already a convicted criminal.'

'Yes,' Henry agreed. He rose to his feet. 'Where may I find this Mr Overton?'

'In the offices at the end of the street. I do not know the number.'

'Thank you. Good day, Mr Percival.'

Percival did not reply.

Henry walked as directed, and found the offices of William Overton after the briefest of questions. He was obliged to wait only twenty minutes in order to see him.

'Come in, Mr Rathbone,' Overton said with courtesy. He was older than Percival. What there was of his hair was grey, almost white, but his lean face was only slightly lined and he moved with ease. 'My clerk says that you are concerned about the deeds which were forged regarding the Gower estate. Terrible tragedy that Judah Dreghorn drowned. I am most deeply sorry. A charming man, of the utmost honesty. What may I do for you?' He waved at the chair opposite his desk, and resumed his own seat.

Henry sat down and told him as briefly as he could.

Overton frowned. 'I am not an expert in forgery, Mr Rathbone. I admit that the document seemed genuine to me, and I have handled a good many in the course of my profession.'

'What was the date on the original document that you had from Geoffrey Gower's safe, compared with the document presented in court, which Mr Percival testified to as forged?'

'They were the same, Mr Rathbone,' Overton replied, frowning. 'Which is why I do not understand the claim that the deeds presented at court were forged.'

'The dates were the same?' Henry swallowed hard. 'You are certain?'

'Of course I am certain.'

'Then what was the purpose of the forgery?'

'I don't know. But most certainly it was not to gain the estate for Ashton Gower. It was his anyway.' Overton leaned forward across his desk. His face was sad and touched with a deep distress. 'It seems to me that someone changed a true document for a false one, but it read exactly the same. The only purpose in that can have been to discredit the genuine deeds. That possibility does not seem to have occurred to anyone at the trial.'

'When were you aware of this, Mr Overton?' Henry was puzzled. Why had this apparently honest man not spoken of what seemed to be a monstrous miscarriage of justice?

'Just over two weeks ago, on the day of Judah Dreghorn's death, he came to me with just the questions you have asked . . .'

Henry felt as if he had been struck a physical blow. Ashton Gower was innocent, and Judah had known it! Why, then, would Gower have killed him?

Or was it not Gower at all, but someone else?

He heard Overton's voice as if from a long way off – words garbled and making no sense.

'I beg your pardon?' he said numbly. 'I'm afraid I did not hear you.'

'You look ill, Mr Rathbone,' Overton repeated. 'May I pour you a glass of brandy? I am afraid this has come as a great shock to you.' He suited his actions to his words, rising to open a cupboard and pour a fairly stiff measure of very good brandy into a glass, and placed it on the edge of the desk where Henry could reach it.

'Thank you.' Henry took it and drank it slowly. He felt its fire inside him and was grateful, but it did not take away the knowledge that filled him with horror.

'Judah was here, and you told him what you told me?' He knew he must sound foolish, but he could not grasp the idea of it.

'Yes,' Overton agreed. 'And he was as horrified as you are. He realised what had happened . . . what he had done, if you like, albeit in complete innocence.'

'Did he . . .' Henry swallowed, '. . . did he say what he intended to do?'

Overton smiled, a small, unhappy gesture full of pity. 'Not precisely. He left here quite early in the afternoon. I think he took the half-past two train to Penrith. He said he intended to see someone, but he did not say whom, nor what he meant to say to them. He would have been in Penrith before half-past three, and perhaps home by five, if he had a good horse. He wished to go to a recital in the village where he lives. It was something to do with his son, who I understand is remarkably gifted.'

'Yes. Yes, he is.' Henry was still thinking in a daze. He tried to imagine what must have been in Judah's mind as he travelled home that day. He knew that Ashton Gower had been innocent. Was it Gower he had intended to see? Or someone else – someone who was guilty?

Had he been too late to see whoever it was before the recital? He would not miss it and disappoint Joshua. Had he planned to see that person after his return home, at the lower crossing? Why there? Closer to the village, but yet private? Closer to the church? The Viking site? Colgrave's house? Or halfway between the estate and someone else's house?

Who was it, and what had transpired? If it was Gower, then had Judah's death been the tragic and idiotic result of an explosion of rage at the injustice of eleven years Gower had spent in prison for a crime he had not committed?

That was possible.

It was equally possible that it was not Ashton Gower at all, but someone else. Peter Colgrave? Or someone who had intended to buy the estate, and been prevented?

One thing was certain, Henry could not leave the matter secret now. The injustice burned like a fire inside him, demanding reparation. If he permitted Ashton Gower to carry the shame of the first crime, and then the fear of the stigma for the second, he would be more guilty than Gower could ever be, because he knew the truth.

'Why did you not do something when you heard of Judah's death, and knew he could not right it?' he asked Overton.

'My dear Rathbone, I have no proof!' Overton replied, turning up his hands. 'I saw the original deed, but it is destroyed now. Only the forgery remains. What could I say, and to whom? Judah Dreghorn could have, but he is dead.'

Of course. Henry should have seen it. Again, he felt as if the ground had risen up and struck him, bruising him bone-deep. It rested with him. There was no one else.

Slowly and a trifle shakily, he rose to his feet, thanked Overton, and made his way back to the station. He sat in the train all the way to Penrith, mulling over anything and everything he could say to the family. None of it stopped the pain in the least, and none of it would be acceptable to them, or dull their anger with him.

He arrived at the house just in time for dinner. It was one of the most miserable of his life. The food was rich, succulent, as if preparing for the taste of the Christmas goose and all the added fare of the season, but it might have been so much stale bread, for any pleasure it gave him.

'We are accomplishing nothing!' Benjamin said miserably. 'Gower is still blackening Judah's name. I heard more of it today and I don't see how we can stop him, except by going to law. Antonia?'

She looked sad and frightened. Henry knew her thoughts were even more of Joshua than for herself. Like any woman who had a child, her will, her emotions, her instinct were all to protect him. She must hurt for Judah also, but her first thought would be for the living. She would perhaps do her real mourning after he was safe.

'If it has to be,' she conceded, but Henry heard the reluctance in her voice, and she turned to him for confirmation that this was the only course.

He hesitated. He would have to tell her the truth, but he dreaded it, and he had not the words yet.

Naomi also looked at Henry, but in her eyes was the question formed by knowledge he had been to Kendal today. He had not told her, he had had no opportunity to speak to her alone, but in that glance she understood. Would she have the courage to risk the love of the family, and help him?

Ephraim filled the silence. 'Only if there's no other way,' he said grimly. 'We won't leave until we've cleared Judah's name from this stupid charge, and proved to everyone that Gower killed him. Then he'll be hanged, and no one will ever repeat anything he said.' He looked at Antonia with a sudden gentleness. 'He was our brother – we'll see justice for his sake. But you are as much a part of our family, and Joshua is the only Dreghorn of the next generation. We would never leave you unprotected.' That was his way of saying that he loved them. Such plain, emotional words were not in his nature.

'Thank you,' Antonia said warmly. 'I know how eager you are to return to your work, and the marvellous places you travel.'

Benjamin smiled. 'When I go back to Palestine we're going to be working in the streets of Jerusalem. We're tracing the way Christ took on Palm Sunday, when he entered in triumph.' His face was lit with a fire that had nothing to do with the chandelier above the table. His mind saw the far-off glory of a different and deeper kind, and for a moment all anger was forgotten. The fire of his emotion burned away lesser, worldly griefs. 'Next we are going to find and make certain of the garden where Mary Magdalene spoke to the risen Christ on Easter Sunday. Can you imagine? We will stand where she stood when He said "Mary", and she knew Him!'

'Perhaps that is where we are all trying to stand,' Naomi said very quietly. 'Only I'm not sure it is a place, I think it is a matter of spirit, it is who you have become.'

There was another long moment's silence.

'But it must be wonderful for you to see it, of course,' she added, as if not to spoil his excitement. She turned to Ephraim. 'Where will you go next?'

He smiled very slightly – an inward pleasure. 'The Rift Valley, in South Africa,' he answered. 'The plants there are different from anywhere else on earth. I expect to see some wonderful animals too, but I shan't be studying them. We could find new foods, new medicines and, of course, the beauty of them is staggering – shapes and colours you never see here.' His voice warmed and became more urgent, and without realising it he was using his hands to echo the shapes he envisioned. 'The variety of creation amazes me more and more every day. It's not just the endless invention of it, it's how every design has unique and absolute purpose! You know . . .' he stopped, realising with a moment of self-consciousness, how his love of it had swept him along. 'Another time,' he finished. 'When we have dealt with Gower.'

Again Henry tried to think how to begin what he must tell them, and his nerve failed. How blunt should he be?

How immediate, or how gentle?

Ephraim had asked Naomi where she was planning to go, and his face was tense, as if he too were struggling with inner turmoil as to what he should say, and how. He feared another rejection. Henry could see that in the tight angles of his body where he sat at the foot of the table. But, like Henry, he was torn in two ways. If he let her go again without saying anything, when would he have another chance? Would he ever? What if she married someone else? The time while they were back here was painful, filled with anger and grief, and yet it would still slip by too quickly for him.

'Not quite a valley,' Naomi answered, and her face, too, lit with the excitement of her inner vision. 'I've heard of a geological phenomenon unlike any other in the world: a gorge so deep you can see almost the whole history of the earth in it.' Her voice quickened. 'The American Indians speak of it as a holy place, but then the whole earth is sacred to them. They treat it with a respect that, if we ever felt, we have forgotten. Perhaps we did anciently? Druid times? But this canyon is so beautiful it is beyond description, and bigger than anything we could imagine. I am going to see that, and climb down it to the river.' She stopped and turned to Antonia. 'I'm sorry. We're all getting carried away with our dreams. What are you going to do? You have a treasure as well, a whole new world to explore. What about Joshua and his music? Are we one day going to be a footnote in history as the family of the English Mozart?'

Antonia blushed, but it was with pleasure. 'Perhaps,' she answered, meeting the mood with hope and optimism of her own. 'As soon as he is old enough we . . . I . . . shall send him to the musical academy in Liverpool. It will be terribly hard to part with him, but it is the only way he will get the education that is right for him. I can go and spend time there now and then, to be near him. It is the right thing to do.' She looked to Henry for his agreement.

He realised how bitterly hard it was going to be for her to bring up such a remarkable child alone, make the decisions, try to be both mother and father to him.

And he was about to add an even greater burden for all of them, but he could not remain silent. He could feel Naomi's eyes on him also – waiting.

He cleared his throat. 'I went to Kendal today,' he began. He could feel his stomach tightening and in spite of the fire and the good food, he was cold.

They were waiting, knowing he would go on and tell them the reason.

'I went to see Percival, the forgery expert—'

'We all know it was forged,' Ephraim interrupted him. 'It's already been proved in court! We need to show that Judah was murdered, and that Gower did it, out of hatred and revenge.'

'For heaven's sake, let him finish!' Benjamin said tartly. 'Why did you go, Henry? What can Percival do to help?'

'I think it would be best if I gave you the whole story I found out,' Henry answered, 'rather than follow my path of discovering that Mr Percival dislikes Gower intensely, so much so that he seems to have allowed his animosity to govern some of his decisions. He admitted he was quick to come to conclusions, and to pass them on to Judah.'

'Are you saying that he was wrong?' Ephraim demanded. 'That is the only fact that matters.'

Henry ignored his manner because he understood the emotions that drove it. 'The date made the property legally Ashton Gower's, but the forgery was so bad it could never have passed for genuine.'

'We know that,' Benjamin agreed. 'Ashton Gower is both a villain and a fool.'

'No,' Henry contradicted him. 'He may have killed Judah, which would make him a villain, but he is not a fool. And if you think about it honestly, you know that.' He leaned forward across the table. 'Percival gave me the name of the original solicitor, who was not called to testify. He did not believe the deeds were forged, but he is not an expert. He was willing to be overruled.'

'Your point, Henry?' Benjamin asked. 'All this means nothing.'

'Yes it does, Benjamin,' Henry replied. 'Overton read the deeds very carefully. He remembered the date in particular.'

Naomi drew in her breath sharply.

'It was the same date as on the forged deeds,' Henry told them.

'That's ridiculous!' Ephraim exploded. 'Why in God's name forge something and make it exactly the same?'

'Because it was obviously a forgery,' Henry answered.

119

'And the original had been destroyed. Naturally, like you, everyone assumed that the original had been different.'

They looked stunned. He turned to each of them, one by one. It was Benjamin who realised the meaning first.

'You mean the original gave the dates that make it Ashton Gower's?' he said incredulously.

'Yes.'

'Oh God! It . . .' he stopped.

Antonia was ashen. 'Judah didn't know!' she said hoarsely. 'He would never lie! Never!'

'Of course he didn't,' Henry agreed instantly. 'But he was, as you say, an honest man, not just outwardly, but of heart and mind deep through. He went back over all he had done to prove to Ashton Gower that he was wrong. And he found what I did. He saw Overton as well, and knew that the land was Gower's. That was the day he died.'

'You mean the day he was murdered!' Ephraim almost choked on the words.

'Yes.'

'What a hideous irony!' Ephraim was white-faced, his hands clenched into fists on the table. 'Gower was right, and Judah could have told him, if Gower hadn't murdered him first. He could have had his name cleared . . .'

'Are we sure it was Gower who killed him?' Henry asked.

Benjamin stared back.

Ephraim sat rigid.

It was Antonia who spoke. 'We are supposing it was he because we also believed he forged the deeds. If he didn't, then perhaps he didn't kill Judah either.'

'Revenge,' Ephraim said quickly. 'If he was innocent, then he had a justified anger. Especially if he believed Judah forged the deeds so we could buy the estate.'

'That's true,' Henry agreed. 'But if Judah was going to tell him the truth, then whoever did forge them – and certainly someone did – that person had a great deal to lose. The case would be opened up again and . . .' Now he had to say it, although it twisted like a knife inside him, '. . . and the estate given back to Gower. And if it proved to be Colgrave who forged the deeds, and since it was in fact he who benefited from the sale, the law would look very seriously at him.'

They all stared at him aghast.

'We bought it legally, at a fair price,' Benjamin said quietly.

'I know that,' Henry answered. 'But you bought it from Colgrave, and it was not his to sell.'

Ephraim looked around the table at each of them in turn. 'That's monstrous!' he burst out. 'Are you saying that if all this is true, then legally the estate, our home, belongs to Ashton Gower after all?'

'Is it true?' Antonia whispered.

Benjamin looked at Henry, hope struggling with knowledge in his eyes.

'Yes,' Henry nodded.

Ephraim struggled to keep hope. 'Unless Gower did kill Judah? If he did, then he can't profit from his crime. Apart from morally, that's the law. He'll be hanged.'

'We didn't consider Peter Colgrave regarding Judah's death,' Benjamin pointed out. 'We were so morally sure that it was Gower. But this makes it different. It also explains why Judah would meet him at the lower crossing. It's only a few hundred yards from Colgrave's house. He might even have been there, and Colgrave followed him out.' He turned to Henry. 'Do you know what Judah was going to do about this?'

'Not from Overton,' Henry replied. 'But I knew Judah, just as you did. He was a man of honour. There is only one thing he could have done.'

Again the silence was painful.

It was Naomi who spoke at last. 'Give it back to Gower?'

'Isn't that what he would do?' Henry asked. 'You knew him. Would he have kept that secret, and stayed living here, with Gower branded a forger, and left penniless?'

It was Antonia who answered. 'No. No, he would never have done that. He couldn't.'

'And he would not have let Colgrave go either,' Benjamin added. 'And Colgrave would have known that.'

Ephraim looked from one to the other of them. 'Would he really have gone to Colgrave's house alone, at that hour of night, to face him with it?'

'No,' Benjamin said with certainty.

'If he was going to give the estate back to Gower, with everything that means,' Henry said slowly, 'his first concern, after doing the right thing, would be to have made some provision for Antonia and Joshua.'

'You can't buy a house at that time of night!' Benjamin said, with something close to derision in his face.

Henry bit his lip. 'Benjamin, with the estate gone, there would be no money with which to buy a house,' he pointed out. 'And since it was a miscarriage of justice of very great proportions, there may have been an inquiry. Gower might not have let it rest in peace. He might have sued—'

Ephraim swore and buried his head in his hands.

'Then who?' Naomi asked. 'Who could help?'

Henry turned to Antonia. 'Who did he trust? Who would be wise, discreet, and unfailingly kind?'

Her eyes were full of tears. 'Apart from you? I don't know.'

Henry found himself blushing at her trust, even after what he had been obliged to tell her. If she had hated him for it, at least for a while, he would not have blamed her. He wished he had anything to offer stronger or of more use than friendship.

'A friend?' Ephraim asked. 'He would know we were all coming, but we don't live here. Who else?'

Benjamin rubbed his hand across his brow. 'Actually, Ephraim, if we lose the estate, we may very well all live here. There'll be no income to support us anywhere else. In fact not even here, come to that. It'll change all our lives.'

'Only if Gower is not guilty,' Ephraim said, but now there was no hope in his eyes. It was as if within himself he knew, he was simply finding the strength to face it. All his passion and dreams were crumbling, towers that had shone in the air only an hour before. If ever he needed courage it was now.

No one bothered to argue with him.

'The Reverend Mr Findheart,' Antonia said, looking at Henry. 'That must have been where he was going. It makes sense now.'

'Then I will go and see him in the morning,' Henry answered. 'Unless you prefer to go?' he looked at Benjamin, then at Ephraim.

'No. Thank you.' Benjamin looked bruised, as if the emotional shock had hurt him physically. 'I had better look at the estate papers, and see what can be saved of ours. If there is anything. Ephraim, will you help?'

Ephraim nodded and reached out his hand to rest it on Benjamin's.

Henry rose to his feet and excused himself. They should be allowed time alone together. There was too much to face for it to be done easily, or quickly. He bade them good night, even though it could not possibly be so, and went upstairs to his room.

The morning was cold with flurries of snow. It was four days until Christmas. Henry had tea and toast alone in the dining room, then put on his greatcoat, hat, scarf and gloves, and set out to walk to the lower crossing of the stream, and the climb beyond.

He would have given anything he could think of not to be bound on this errand. The land was beautiful, great sweeping hills mantled in snow, black rocks making patterns through the white, steep sides plunging to the water. Wind-riven, the ragged skies were scattered with clouds and light, casting swift-moving shadows over the earth. Trees were stark, soft flakes blurring the edges even as he looked.

The estate itself had a wealth and a beauty it would tear the heart to leave behind. The Dreghorns had been good husbanders of its wealth. They would leave it far richer than Geoffrey Gower had. But Henry had no doubt for even a second, a passing instant, that this is what Judah had begun, and would have finished had not Colgrave killed him. He had a wrong to undo, whatever the cost. He would have made no excuse.

Henry reached the stream, swift-flowing under the flat stones that stretched across, like planks. He could never forget that this was where Judah had died.

He set out across the narrow way, taking small steps, balancing with his arms out a little. He did not care if he looked foolish.

The stone church with its squared tower was visible as soon as he rounded the corner of the hill, with the large vicarage beyond it, the orchard trees bare now, coated only with a dusting of snow. The lake water shimmered in grey and silver, always moving.

Henry trudged through the unbroken white, leaving his footprints to mark his way. At the gate he stopped, fumbling for the latch. It was indecently early to visit an elderly man. Perhaps he had been precipitate? He was still standing uncertainly when the front door opened and he saw the vicar regarding him with interest. He was thin and bent, with white hair blowing in the gusts of wind.

'Good morning,' Henry said, a trifle embarrassed at being caught staring.

'Good morning, sir,' Findheart answered with a smile. 'Would you like a cup of tea? Or even breakfast?'

Henry undid the gate latch and went in, closing it carefully behind him.

'Thank you,' he accepted.

He was inside with his wet shoes and coat taken by an ancient housekeeper, and sitting by the fire in the dining room in his stocking feet with hot tea, toast and honey, before he approached the subject for which he had come.

'Mr Findheart, I was a close friend of Judah Dreghorn's . . .'

'I know,' Findheart said mildly. 'He spoke of you, the night he was here, just before he died.'

Henry was grateful to be helped; it would be hard enough. 'I went to Kendal and spoke to Mr Overton. I know now what Judah learned. Is that what he said to you that evening?'

'Yes.' Findheart added nothing, but he kept smiling, his blue eyes infinitely gentle. It was a confidence he was still not going to break. Henry would have to spell it out.

Henry sighed. 'He learned that Ashton Gower was innocent, and the estate really did belong to him. Judah was going to give it back, wasn't he?'

'Yes. It was the only honourable thing to do,' Findheart

agreed. 'Do have some more tea. You must be cold.'

Henry accepted. 'Did he ask you to care for Antonia, and her son, if he should be unable to?'

'He did. But of course that will only be necessary should they carry through Judah's wishes.' He did not make it a question, but in effect, it was.

'Yes, they will,' Henry said softly. 'They are Dreghorns too. But it will leave them all without means. Benjamin will have to give up his archaeology in the Holy Land. Ephraim will not be able to go back to Africa, and Naomi too will have to remain here in England. I am not aware if Nathaniel left her with anything, but I imagine it would be only what income he had from the estate. And, of course, there are Antonia and Joshua. They will be without a home or means of any sort.'

'I know,' Findheart said. 'I have given it much thought. The answer seems to me quite clear. I have served in this church for thirty years, and loved it dearly, but it is time for me to retire. I am getting old.' He smiled ruefully. He must have been long past eighty. His eyes were bright but his skin was withered and his hands were veined in blue. 'I have not the strength for the pastoral work that I used to have,' he went on. 'The people need and deserve a younger man, one better able to ride to the sick in the outlying farms and dales, one who can answer their call for the frightened, the sick and the lonely, the grieving and the troubled, at any hour. Benjamin Dreghorn is ordained to that office. He may take my place, and serve God here.'

He lifted his hand in a small gesture. 'The vicarage is large and warm, well suited for a family. There would be room for Antonia and Joshua, and for Ephraim too, if he wishes, and for Naomi. It would shelter them all. There are vegetables in the garden and fruit in the orchard, if anyone will labour to make it yield.' He smiled apologetically. 'It is not the new and exciting botany of Africa, but it will feed the people, and to spare. And there is honey in the hives, and fish in the stream and in the lake.'

Henry was grateful, and amazed at the simplicity of it. In a bolt of memory like a physical shock he heard again Naomi's words that the garden where Mary Magdalene recognised the risen Christ was not a physical place, but one of the mind, and of the spirit.

'Thank you,' he said aloud. 'I will tell them.' He was unsure how to say to this gentle, generous-hearted man that they may find the loss too profound to be graceful about it for some time yet.

Findheart nodded. 'Of course,' he agreed. 'Of course. But I shall make all ready for them, at least for Antonia, if that is what she chooses. You are a good friend, Mr Rathbone. Your presence will make it less difficult for them than it might have been. Judah Dreghorn was a man of the utmost integrity of heart. No other course is open to those who would be his heirs.'

Henry found his throat suddenly constricted and his eyes prickled with tears. Sitting in this quiet vicarage with the fire burning gently in the hearth and the snow drifting pale flurries outside, he was more truly aware of how much he missed Judah, not just his company, his laughter, but the certainty of honour in him, that truth inside that was never tainted.

He sat for another half-hour, learning more about the church and the vicarage and what abundant room it offered for all of them. Then he thanked Findheart, put on his shoes, now nearly dry, and his coat, scarf and gloves, and set out to retrace his steps, already vanished in the snow.

It was nearly eleven in the morning by the time he was back in the house. Benjamin met him in the hallway. He looked tired, as if he had slept little.

'Yes,' Henry said immediately. 'Judah went to Findheart.'

'What can Findheart do? He's the vicar of a village church, and must be closer to ninety than eighty.' There was despair in Benjamin's voice, edging on bitterness.

Henry plunged in. He was aware of Antonia coming down the stairs with Joshua on her heels.

'Give you his living at the church,' Henry replied simply. 'You are ordained to the priesthood. You can serve God better here than unearthing the stones of the past in Jerusalem. Here you are needed. And the vicarage is large enough to accommodate you all, and with room to spare.'

'All?' Benjamin was startled.

'There will be no means from the estate to provide anything else,' Henry pointed out. 'There is no heritage for any of you, Benjamin, except the one nobody can spend or take from you, a name of honour above that of any other I know. Judah Dreghorn was a man of integrity like a star that cannot be dimmed. There was no shadow in him.'

Antonia caught her breath and buried her face in her hands. Very slowly she sat down on the stairs, and Joshua put his arms around her.

Ephraim came out of the study doorway where apparently he had been listening. Naomi came from the other direction, looking at Henry, then at Ephraim.

'Of course,' Benjamin said at last. 'I'm sorry. I wasn't thinking. Yes, we will do very well there. Ephraim?'

It was too soon. Ephraim looked stunned, like a man who has seen darkness come at midday, and cannot believe it.

Naomi walked over to him, and slowly his eyes met hers.

He did not know what to do, he was so hurt.

Antonia lifted her face. 'And I'm proud that he knew we would do the same thing,' she said quietly. 'He did not doubt us either, not any of us. And he was right. We will do what he would have. The land and the house and everything in it will go back to Ashton Gower, because it is his by all the moral laws. What we lose if we do this will be nothing compared with what we would lose if we did not. We would lose ourselves, and we would lose the love Judah would have felt for us, and the right to belong to him.'

Ephraim looked at her with a sudden burning of pride, then at Naomi standing in front of him. 'I can understand Gower,' he said with difficulty. 'He has suffered appallingly, and unjustly. He's a miserable swine, but perhaps in his place I'd have been no better.'

Naomi smiled at him with a total and glowing warmth. 'Probably worse,' she agreed, but she said it so gently that he blushed with deep, almost painful joy.

The following day it was accomplished at law. They all took the train to Penrith and with Ashton Gower present, swore to the events as they now knew them. Overton had been sent for from Kendal, and he also testified to his knowledge of Judah's discovery, and his intentions.

The police were advised of what seemed now inevitably to have been Colgrave's part in it. They instituted investigations, which they had no doubt would lead to his arrest for both the forgery and the murder of Judah Dreghorn.

'A man of the utmost honour,' the magistrate said of Judah, speaking with intense feeling. He looked at Joshua, who had asked to be with them. 'You have a proud heritage, young man. You can look anyone in England in the eye, and bow your knee to no one, except the Queen.'

'Yes, sir,' Joshua answered quietly. 'I knew that before.'

'I imagine you did,' the magistrate said with a nod. 'At least you believed it. But it takes a bitter test of all that he has to make a hero like your father. Sometimes we bring to a struggle or a cause the gifts we see most clearly, a courage, a strength or a charm others have told us we have. But often we find more is asked of us than that, more than we intended or thought we possessed. We are asked to offer that which we thought dearest, to forgive what seemed unpardonable, to face what we feared the most and endure it. Sometimes we have to travel to the last step a path that was not of our choosing. But I promise you this, young man, it will lead to a greater joy in the end. The difficulty is that the end is beyond our sight, it is a matter of faith, not of knowledge.'

Joshua nodded, but he did not know what to say.

Antonia rested her hand on his shoulder. Her face was calm through her tears, but in her eyes was a fierce pride, and a certainty of understanding.

Ephraim put his arm around Naomi and she did not move away.

Benjamin offered his hand to Ashton Gower.

Slowly Gower reached across and clasped it. 'He's right,' he said with something like surprise, as if he were watching a light breaking across the horizon. 'Judah Dreghorn was a man of the highest honour. I'll say that to anyone. You all are. I don't know that we'll ever be friends, there's too much hard history between us, and I've said and done ill by you. But by the Lord in Heaven, I admire you!' He turned and offered his hand to Ephraim.

Ephraim took it and held it hard, even with warmth.

'I'm sorry,' he said. 'I spoke badly of you, and it was untrue.'

Gower nodded. 'Christmas in three days,' he said. 'Chance to start over. Do it better this time.' He looked at Henry. 'Thank you,' he added simply.

Headline hopes that you have enjoyed reading Anne Perry's A CHRISTMAS VISITOR and invites you to sample SHOULDER THE SKY, out now from Headline Review.

Chapter One

It was shortly after three in the afternoon. Joseph Reavley was half asleep in the April sun, his back to the pale clay wall of the trench, when he heard the angry voices.

'They be moi boots, Tucky Nunn, an' you know that well as Oi do! Yours be over there, wi' holes in 'em!' It was Plugger Arnold, a seasoned soldier of twenty, big-boned, a son of the village blacksmith. He had been in Flanders since the outbreak of war last August. Although he was angry, he kept his voice low. He knew it carried in the afternoon stillness when the men snatched the three or four hours of sleep they could. The German trenches were only seventy yards away across this stretch of the Ypres Salient. Anyone foolish enough to reach a hand up above the parapet would be likely to get it shot. The snipers seldom needed a second chance. Added to which, getting yourself injured on purpose was a court-martial offence.

Tucky Nunn, nineteen and new this far forward, was standing on the duckboards that floored the trench. They were there to keep the men's feet above the icy water that sloshed around, but this seldom worked. The water level was too high. Every time you thought the ground was drying out at last, it rained again.

'Yeah?' Tucky said, his eyebrows raised. 'Fit me perfect, they do. Didn't see your name on 'em. Must 'ave wore off.' He grinned, making no move to bend and unlace the offending boots and hand them back.

Plugger was sitting half sideways on the fire-step. A few yards away the sentry was standing with his back to them, staring through the periscope over the wire and mud of no man's land. He could not afford to lose concentration even for a moment, regardless of what went on behind him.

'They's moi boots,' Plugger said between his teeth. 'Take 'em off yer soddin' feet an' give 'em back to me, or Oi'll take 'em off yer and give yer to the rats!'

Tucky bounced on the balls of his feet, hunching his shoulders a little. 'You want to try?' he invited.

Doughy Ward crawled out of his dugout, fully dressed as they all were: webbing and rifle with bayonet attached. His fair-skinned face was crumpled with annoyance at being robbed of any part of his few hours of sleep. He glared at Joseph. ' "Thou shalt not steal." Isn't that right, Chaplain?'

It was a demand that even here in the mud and the cold, the boredom and sporadic violence, Joseph should do his job and stand for the values of justice that must remain, or all this would sink into a purposeless hell. Without right and wrong there was no sanity.

'Oi didn't steal them!' Tucky said angrily. 'They were—' He did not finish the sentence because Plugger hit him, a rolling blow that caught the side of his jaw as he ducked and struck back.

There was no point in shouting at them, and the sound would carry. Added to which, Joseph did not want to let the whole trench know that there was a discipline problem. Both men could end up on charges, and that was not the way for a chaplain to resolve anything. He moved forward, careful to avoid being struck himself, and grasped hold of Tucky, taking him off balance and knocking him against the uprights that held the trench wall.

'The Germans are that way!' he said tartly, jerking his head back towards the parapet and no man's land beyond.

Plugger was up on his feet, slithering in the mud on the duckboards, his socks filthy and sodden wet. 'Good oidea to send him over the top, Captain, where he belongs! But not in moi boots!' He was floundering towards them, arms flailing as if to carry on the fight.

Joseph stepped between them, risking being caught by both, which would make charges unavoidable. 'Stop it!' he ordered briskly. 'Take the boots off, Nunn!'

'Thank you, Chaplain,' Plugger responded with a smile of satisfaction.

Tucky stood unmoving, his face set, ignoring the blood. 'They ain't his boots oither!' he said sullenly, his eyes meeting Joseph's.

A man appeared around the dogleg corner. No stretch of the trench was more than ten or twelve yards long, to prevent shellfire taking out a whole platoon of men – or in case a German raiding party made it through the wire. The trenches were steep-sided, shored up against mud slides, and barely wide enough for two men to pass each other. The man coming was tall and lean, with wide shoulders, and he walked with a certain elegance, even on the slopping duckboards. His face was dark, long-nosed, and there was a wry humour in it.

'Early for tea, aren't you?' he asked, his eyes going from one to another.

Tucky and Plugger reluctantly stood to attention. 'Yes, Major Wetherall,' they said almost in unison.

Sam Wetherall glanced down at Plugger's stocking feet, his eyebrows raised. 'Thinking of creeping up on the cook, are you? Or making a quick recce over the top first?'

'Soon as Oi get moi boots back from that thievin' sod, Oi'll put 'em on again,' Plugger replied, gesturing towards Tucky.

'I'd wash them first if I were you,' Sam advised with a smile.

'Oi will,' Plugger agreed. 'Oi don't want to catch nothin'!'

'I meant your feet,' Sam corrected him.

Tucky Nunn roared with laughter, in spite of the bruise darkening on his jaw where Plugger had caught him.

'Whose boots are they?' Joseph asked, smiling as well.

'Moine!' both men said together.

'Whose boots are they?' Joseph repeated.

There was a moment's silence.

'Oi saw 'em first,' Plugger answered.

'You didn't take them,' Tucky pointed out. 'If you 'ad, you'd 'ave them now, wouldn't you?'

'Come on, Solomon.' Sam looked at Joseph, his mouth pulled into an ironic twist.

'Right,' Joseph said decisively. 'Left boot, Nunn. Right boot, Arnold.'

There was considerable grumbling, but Tucky took off the right boot and passed it over, reaching for one of the worn boots where Plugger had been sitting.

'Shouldn't have had them off now anyway,' Sam said disapprovingly. 'You know better than that. What if Fritz'd made a sudden attack?'

Plugger's eyebrows shot up, his blue eyes wide open. 'At half-past three in the afternoon? It's tea-toime in a minute. They may be soddin' Germans, but they're not uncivilized. They still got to eat an' sleep, same as us.'

'You stick your head up above the parapet, and you'll find he's nowhere near asleep, I promise you,' Sam warned.

Tucky was about to reply when there was a shouting about twenty yards along the line, and a moment later a young soldier lurched around the corner, his face white. He stared at Sam.

'One of your sappers has taken half his hand off!' he said, his voice high-pitched and jerky.

'Where is he, Charlie?' Joseph said quickly. 'We'll get him to the first-aid post.'

Sam was rigid. 'Who is it?' He started forward, pushing ahead of both of them, ignoring the rats scattering in both directions.

Charlie Gee swivelled and went on his heels; Joseph stopped to duck into the connecting trench leading back to the second line, then picked out a first-aid pack in case they needed more than the field dressing the wounded man should be carrying himself.

When he caught up with them Sam was bent over, one arm around a man sitting on the duckboards. The sapper was rocking back and forth, clutching the stump of his hand to his chest, scarlet blood streaming from it.

Joseph had lost count of how many wounded and dead he had seen, but each man's horror was new and real, and it looked as if in this case the man might have lost a good deal of his right hand.

Sam was ashen, his jaw clenched so tight the muscles stood out like cords. 'We have to see it, Corliss!' His voice shook in spite of everything he could do to steady it. 'We have to stop the bleeding!' He looked at Joseph, his eyes desperate.

Joseph tore open the dressing and, speaking gently to the injured man, took his hand and, without examining it, pressed the bandage and the lint over the streaming wound, then bound it as well as he could. He had very little idea how many fingers were left.

'Come on, ol' feller,' Charlie said, trying to help Corliss to his feet. 'Oi'll get you back to the doc's and they'll do it for you proper.'

Sam climbed to his feet and pulled Joseph aside as Charlie and Corliss stumbled past.

'Joe, can you go with them?' Sam said urgently. He swallowed, gulping. 'Corliss is in a hell of a state. He's been on the edge of funking it for days. I've got to find out what happened, put in a report, but the medics'll ask him what caused it . . . Answer for him, will you?' He stopped, but it was painfully apparent he wanted to say more.

Suddenly Joseph understood. Sam was terrified the man had injured himself deliberately. Some men panicked, worn down by fear, cold and horror, and put their hands up above the parapet precisely so a sniper would get them. A hand maimed was 'a Blighty one', and they got sent home. But if it was self-inflicted, it was considered cowardice in the face of the enemy. It warranted a court martial, and possibly even the death sentence. Corliss's nerves may have snapped. It happened to men sometimes. Anything could trigger it off: the incessant noise of bombardment, the dirt, body lice; for some it was waking in the night with rats crawling over your body – or worse, your face. The horror of talking one moment to a man you had grown up with, the next seeing him blown to bits, perhaps armless and legless but still alive, taking minutes of screaming in agony to die – it was more than some could take. For others it was the guilt of knowing that your bullets or your bayonet were doing the same to a German you had never met, but who was your own age, and essentially just like you – warm, breathing, laughing, eating. Sometimes they crept over no man's land at night and swapped food. Occasionally you could even hear them singing. Different things broke different men. Corliss was a sapper. His nerve could have gone at the claustrophobia of crawling inside the tunnels under the earth, the terror of being buried alive.

'Help him,' Sam begged. 'I can't go . . . and they won't believe me anyway.'

'Of course.' Joseph did not hesitate. He grasped Sam's arm for an instant, then turned and made his way back over the duckboards to the opening of the communication trench. Charlie Gee and Corliss were far enough ahead of him to be out of sight round one of the numerous dogleg bends. He hurried, his feet slithering on the wet boards. In some places chicken wire had been tacked over them to give a grip, but no one had bothered here. He must catch up with them before they reached the supply trench and someone else started asking questions.

Morale was Joseph's job – to keep up courage and belief, to help the injured, too often the dying. He wrote letters home for those who could not, either through injury or inability to put into words emotions that overwhelmed them, and for which there was no common understanding. He tried to offer some meaning to pain almost beyond bearing. They were already in the ninth month of the bitterest and most all-consuming war the world had ever seen.

To begin with they had believed it would be over by Christmas, but that had been December 1914. Now it was April 1915, the British Expeditionary Force of almost one hundred thousand men was wiped out, either dead or injured, and it was desperate that new recruits were found. Kitchener had called for a million men, and they would be fresh, healthy, not having endured a winter in the open in the unceasing cold and rain. They would not have lice, swollen and peeling feet, or a dozen other miseries to debilitate them.

Joseph crossed the reserve trench and saw men moving. A soldier was singing to himself 'It's a Long Way to Tipperary' as he poured water out of a petrol can, wrinkling his nose at the smell. He balanced the dixie tin over a precarious arrangement of candles to heat it. He raised a hand to Joseph and smiled without distracting his attention from his task.

The men in this segment were from the Cambridgeshire villages around Joseph's home of Selbourne St Giles. Most of them knew each other by their local nicknames. Joseph was thirty-six, and for the years leading up to the war had been a lecturer in Biblical languages at St John's College in Cambridge. Before that he had been in the ministry. He knew most of these men's families. His own youngest sister, Judith, was twenty-four, older than many of these.

He thought of her with a twisting confusion of emotions. He was intensely proud that she had volunteered to use her one distinctive skill, driving, to come here and work wherever she could help. She had been both a joy and a menace on the roads at home, but here she coped with the mud, the breakdowns, the long hours and the horror of wounded and dying men with a courage he had not known she possessed.

The trench was climbing a bit, and drier. The slit of sky overhead was blue, with a thin drift of clouds, like mares' tails.

Joseph was afraid for Judith in many ways. The obvious danger of injury or even death was only a part of it. There was also the vulnerability of the mind and heart to the destruction around her: the drowning in pain, the loss of so many young men, and the inability of the ambulances to do more than carry them from one place to another, very often too late. He knew the questions that tormented his own mind. No sane person could be wholehearted about war, not if they had seen it. It was one thing to stand in England in the early spring with the hedgerows beginning to bud, wild birds singing and daffodils in the gardens and along the banks under the trees, and speak of the nobility of war. It was an idea, even at times a noble one. Most people despised the thought of surrender.

Out here it was a reality. You were always cold – frozen at times – and usually wet. All waking hours were occupied with monotonous routine: carrying, cleaning, digging, shoring up walls, trying to heat food and find drinkable water. You were always tired. And then there were the short interludes of horror: fear crawling in your stomach, shattering noise, and the blood and the pain, men dead – young men you had known and liked. Some would still be crippled long after the war passed into history; the nightmares would never be over for them.

And maybe Germany had invaded 'poor little' Belgium, and a matter of honour rested on it. Invasion was wrong; that was the one thing about which there was no question in anyone's mind. But the few German soldiers Joseph had seen were in every way but uniform indistinguishable from the Englishmen beside him. They were young, tired, dirty, and confused like everyone else.

When a successful raiding party captured someone and brought him back, Joseph had often been chosen to question the prisoner because before the war he had spent time in Germany and spoke the language not only fluently but with pleasure. Looking back on those times now was a wrenching, muddled sort of pain. He had been treated with such courtesy, laughed with them, shared their food. It was the land of Beethoven and Goethe, of science and philosophy and vast myths and dreams. How could they now be doing this to each other?

Joseph turned the last corner, and up a couple of steps he caught up with Charlie Gee and Corliss, but the trench was still too narrow for him to help. Two men could barely walk side by side, let alone three abreast.

The main dressing station was in a tent a few yards away. At least it was dry, and no more of a target than any other structure. It was quite spacious inside. After a bad raid they had to deal with dozens of men, moving them in and out as rapidly as ambulances could take them back to proper hospitals. Just now there was a lull. Only two men were inside, grey-faced, their uniforms blood-stained, waiting to be moved.

Charlie Gee gave a shout, and a young doctor appeared, saw Corliss and immediately went to him.

'Come on, we'll get that fixed up,' he said calmly. His eyes flickered to Joseph and then back again. It was easy enough to see in his haggard, hollow-eyed face the fear that a hand wound was self-inflicted.

Joseph moved forward quickly. 'We did what we could to stem the bleeding, Doctor, but I don't know exactly what happened. He's a sapper; I imagine something collapsed underground. Maybe one of the props gave way.'

The doctor's face eased a little. 'Right.' He turned back to Corliss and took him inside.

Joseph thanked Charlie Gee and watched him amble back up the connecting trench towards the front line again.

An ambulance pulled up, a square-bodied Ford Model T, a bit like a delivery van. It was open at the front, and with a closed part at the back, which could carry up to five men laid out in stretchers, more if they were sitting up. The driver jumped out. He was a broad-shouldered young man with short hair that sat up on the crown of his head. He saluted Joseph, then looked at the more seriously injured of the two men waiting, whose right leg was heavily splinted.

'Don't need ter carry yer,' he said cheerfully. 'Reckon an arm round yer and yer'll be fine. 'Ave yer in 'ospital in an hour, or mebbe less, if Jerry don't make too much of a mess o' them roads. Cut 'em up terrible around Wipers, they 'ave. An' 'Ellfire Corner's a right shootin' gallery. Still, we'll cut up a few o' them, an' all. Looks broke all right.' He regarded the splinted leg cheerfully. 'Reckon that's a Blighty one, at least for a while, eh?'

'Oi'll be back!' the soldier said quietly. 'Oi've seen a lot worse than broken legs.'

'So've I, mate, so've I.' The ambulance driver pursed his lips. 'But this'll do for now. Now let's be 'avin' yer.'

Joseph moved forward. 'Can I help?' he offered.

'Blimey! 'E don' need the last rites yet, Padre. It's only 'is leg! The rest of 'im's right as rain,' the ambulance driver said with a grin. 'Still – I s'pose yer could take the other side of 'im, stop 'im fallin' that way, like?'

A quarter of an hour later Joseph was refreshed by really quite drinkable tea. Unlike in the front trenches, there was plenty of it, almost too hot to drink, and strong enough to disguise the other tastes in the water.

He had almost finished it when a car drove up. It was a long, low-slung Aston Martin, and out of it stepped a slim, upright young man with very fair hair and a fresh complexion. He wore uniform, but with no rank. He ignored Joseph and went straight into the tent, leaving the flap open. He stopped in front of the surgeon, who was now tidying up his instruments, almost at attention.

'Eldon Prentice, war correspondent,' he announced.

Joseph followed him in. 'Bit dangerous up here, Mr Prentice,' he said, carefully not looking towards Corliss, who was lying on one of the palliasses, his bandaged hand already stained with blood again. 'I'd go a bit further back, if I were you,' he added.

Prentice stared at him, his chin lifted a little, his blunt face smooth, perfectly certain of himself. 'And who are you, sir?'

'Captain Reavley, chaplain,' Joseph replied.

'Good. You can probably give me some accurate first-hand information,' Prentice said. 'Or at least second-hand.'

Joseph heard the challenge in his voice. 'It's cold, wet and dirty,' he replied, looking at Prentice's clean trousers and only faintly dusty boots. 'And, of course, you'll have to walk! And carry your rations. You do have rations, don't you?'

Prentice looked at him curiously. 'A chaplain is just the sort of man I'd like to talk to. You'd be able to give me a unique view of how the men feel, what their thoughts and fears are.'

Joseph instinctively disliked the man. There was an arrogance in his manner that offended him. 'Perhaps you haven't heard, Mr Prentice, but priests don't repeat what people tell them, if it's of any importance.'

Prentice smiled. 'Yes, I imagine you have heard a great many stories of pain, fear and horror, Captain. Some of them must be heart-rending, and leave you feeling utterly helpless. After all, what can you do?' It was a rhetorical question, and yet he seemed to be waiting for an answer.

He had described exactly Joseph's dilemma, and the emotions that most troubled him, awakening a feeling of inadequacy, even failure. There was so little he could do to help, and even then it was trivial, but he was damned if he would admit it to this correspondent. The feeling of inadequacy caused too deep a hurt to speak of, even to himself.

'Nothing that is really your concern, Mr Prentice,' he said aloud. 'A man's troubles, whatever they are, are private to him. That is one of the few decencies we can grant.'

Prentice stood still for a moment, and then he turned very slowly and looked at Corliss. 'What happened to him?' he asked curiously. 'Bad ammunition exploded and took off his fingers?'

'He was down the saps,' Joseph said tartly.

Prentice looked blank.

'Tunnels,' Joseph explained. 'The intention is that the Germans won't know where the tunnels are. They get within a yard or two of their trenches, then lay mines. If a mine had exploded there'd be nothing left of any of them.'

'He's a sapper? I hear that men reaching their hands above the parapet level sometimes get hit by snipers.' Prentice was watching Joseph intently.

Joseph drew in breath to reply, and then changed his

mind. Prentice was a war correspondent, like any other. They all pooled their information anyway – he knew that. He had seen them meeting together in the cafés when he had been behind the lines in one of the towns at Brigade Headquarters, or even further back at Divisional Headquarters. Nobody could see everything; the differences in their stories depended upon interpretation, what they selected and how they wrote it up.

There was movement at the entrance, and a sergeant came in. He saluted Joseph, ignored Prentice and spoke to the doctor, then went to Corliss.

'What happened, soldier?'

Corliss stared up at him. 'Not sure, sir. Bit of the wall fell in. Something landed on my hand.'

'What? A pick?'

'Could be, I suppose.'

'Hurts?'

'Yes, sir, but not too much. I expect I'll be all right.'

'Sapper without 'is fingers is not much use. Looks like a Blighty one.' The sergeant pushed out his lip dubiously, but his voice was not unkind.